A TIME FOR WAR
Spiritual Battle Strategies
For The Christian

By Pastor Frank Solberg

Solid Rock Books, Inc.
979 Young Street, Suite E
Woodburn, OR 97071
Printed in the United States of America

ACKNOWLEDGMENT

I am most grateful for the long and demanding hours of dedication given by Rev. Donald Hall in the editing of this book. The hours of discussion of theological points will be long remembered and treasured. I thank Betty Graves for her financial contribution.

I dedicate this book to my wife, Shirley, who has patiently put up with the many hours devoted to it. She is the other half of the ministry and has not received the credit she deserves. Her contribution to this ministry is invaluable and I now wish it had been more evident in these writings. I truly praise God for her and her dedication to the ministry.

Pastor Frank Solberg
9911 N.W. 14th Court
Vancouver, WA 98685
(206) 573-3307

TABLE OF CONTENTS

INTRODUCTION

Deliverance - just the mention of the word conjures up frightening remembrances of horror movies such as The Exorcist (as if one was not enough, we got Exorcist II) plus a whole genre of best-sellers to give nightmares to the stoutest of heart. Not only in the secular realm but among Christian witnesses we have heard such frightening stories that no sensible saint would pray for such a ministry. (Imagine carrying buckets into a meeting so that the afflicted could vomit out their demons.)

I was no different than the vast majority of pastors. I thought it most likely that demon activity was limited to the occult and to spirit-worshipping peoples overseas. I had never seen a demon possessed person and I hoped to never see one. I had once prayed for the gifts of healing because I could see many sick among God's people and I truly desired them to be healed. But a deliverance ministry - no thank you! And besides, Christians couldn't have demons anyway, could they?

One night a distraught mother called me to her home to minister to her son. When I arrived I was brought, ready or not, face to face with the forces of hell. Whether I wanted it or not, it was get into deliverance or get out of ministry. I had no preparation other than a fast reading of Don Basham's book "Deliver Us From Evil." But we engaged the enemy and in due course the victory was won.

Thus I was thrust into a ministry that has surprised me on two counts: one, the problem is far more extensive than any secular writer has shown and, two, the problem is far less frightening than most secular writers would like.

I don't wish to lessen the truly frightening possibilities of demon possession. I believe most, if not all, murderers (without question, all serial killers) are demon possessed. Suicides and probably the severely accident-prone are being pressed to their death by spirits of death and destruction. This can be terrifying. However, in the general population, the extremes of such possession are rare. It may even be possible that Satan is not too happy to be so obviously exposed.

It is the extent of less blatant, but still quite compulsive, behavior that I found so amazing. I don't think I would have been so surprised if it had been among the worldly only but to find earnest believers struggling helplessly with recurrent sin patterns is a continuing source of wonder. Over and over again, in this ministry, desperate Christians have come to find that their struggle to overcome rage, lust, lying and a multitude of other problems had its source not in a peculiarity of their make-up but in the destructive work of demonic invasion.

God has graciously shown me how through the provisions of the Cross and the powerful working of the Holy Spirit the captives can be freed. It is for this reason I have written this book: I want to see the increasing fulfillment of Isaiah's prophecy quoted by Jesus concerning His ministry:

> The Spirit of the Lord is upon me, because he hath anointed me to preach the gospel to the poor; he hath sent me to heal the brokenhearted, to preach deliverance to the captives, and recovering of sight to the blind, to set at liberty them that are bruised, to preach the acceptable year of the Lord. [Luke 4:18,19]

The first part of the book recounts my own destructive walk in life until God got my full attention. I was traditionally trained for the pastorate but not at all prepared for spiritual warfare as it began to come during the second year of the pastorate in Southwest Idaho. I have detailed how we have been led, step by step by the Holy Spirit, into a full-time ministry of non-violent deliverance and inner healing.

The second part of the book deals with the historical aspects of spiritual warfare from a biblical standpoint. Here it is seen that Satan has always worked to thwart the purposes of God and that many of the events were his attempts to destroy the people of God. I attempt to establish that warfare and satanic purpose has not abated in our time. We are faced with the final onslaughts of an implacable foe. But we shall overcome - by the blood of the Lamb and the word of our testimony!

The final part of the book is designed to help believers to be prepared for the battles. It shows how to engage victoriously in non-violent deliverance. The more common unclean spirits are identified and terminology is defined so that the enemy cannot easily bring confusion when deliverance is attempted. It is my earnest conviction that the ordinary Christian can bring about successful deliverance, however I am not saying that everyone is to have a deliverance ministry. Just as all believers are to witness and evangelize, not all believers are evangelists. So it is that not all are to give themselves to this type of ministry. We must all be ready to engage in any aspect of ministry in which Jesus Christ would be involved.

Beloved, it is time for war! For far too long the Church has acquiesced to ideas that precluded the possibility of demonic activity. Satan has taken every advantage and many believers are convinced that even God cannot help them in their distress. It is a lie! God has means that we have not yet utilized. The provisions of the Cross and the ministry of the Holy Spirit are sufficient to meet and defeat the enemy on his own ground. We can put on the full armor of God and be victorious. Gird up, Christian soldiers - it is time for war!

PART I: (BIOGRAPHICAL)

CHAPTER 1

CALLED TO THE FRONT

A man once said to me, "The Lutheran Church is so bound with tradition and doctrine that the Holy Spirit cannot function within it." The obvious implication was it was not possible for God, the Holy Spirit, to function in the Lutheran Church. I take exception to that generalization because I know the Holy Spirit touched me early in my life.

At the age of sixteen I was received into full membership in the Lutheran Church through the rite of confirmation. In that rite, the pastor lays his hands upon the head of each candidate and invokes a blessing. When the pastor laid his hands upon my head something happened. I did not know then what it was. I realize now what I experienced was the outpouring of the Holy Spirit and with that outpouring came a call to the Lord's ministry.

As powerful as it was, I resisted the call to the ministry for the next sixteen years as the call of the world occupied my mind. The call to ministry was also set aside by military service during World War II. Thirty-five missions flown over occupied Europe in a heavy bomber drove me deeper into the ways of the world and farther away from God's service.

In 1956 I experienced another touch of God. I was employed as a heavy equipment operator on a new highway being constructed through the little town of Cathlamet, Washington. My relationship with the Lord at that time was not right. I was troubled in my soul and desired to correct my life style. Cathlamet was a sleepy town on the road down the Columbia River to the Pacific Coast and offered very little entertainment for a lonely construction worker many miles from home. Two taverns and a movie theater were the main sources.

One night, bored with the tavern, I decided to take in a mid-week movie. I did not check to see what was playing, I just desired to get my mind off things that were troubling me. It was no coincidence I chose that night to attend a movie since it was the only movie I ever attended in the four months I spent in that town. God chose that night and that movie to touch me.

The movie, "A Man Called Peter," was a portrayal of the life story of Peter Marshall, a prominent minister and chaplain of the U.S. Senate during World War II. Excerpts from his sermons were used in the movie. As God's word came from the movie screen, God touched me in a powerful way. I left the theater convicted - if at all possible, I would answer God's call to the ministry.

My life in military service and the working world had convinced me the churches I attended and the pastors I heard failed to reach the needs of those in the pews. I felt they failed to preach and teach the reality of life. It was my impression that much of what passed as preaching never went beyond the theoretical level. Ideals were set forth which never reached down to the level of the man and woman seated in the pew who must fight the daily battles of life in the working world.

I resolved if I ever stood in the pulpit to preach, I would preach to all the other Frank Solbergs seated before me. I would preach the Law of God in all of its severity and the Gospel in all of its beauty and comfort. Little did I realize that such preaching and teaching leads one deep into the truths of living the sanctified life. Nor did I realize then how ill-equipped the average Christian was to cope with the deeper concepts of the sanctified life.

A few months after the incident in the movie theater I was seriously injured in a construction accident. Unable to work for a year, I was confronted with the wretchedness and futility of my life. My experiences in World War II, flying missions over Europe without a strong relationship with the Lord, had been devastating. And now trying to find my niche in the post-war era was frustrating. Just when it seemed that things were beginning to fall into place, my whole world was shattered by the accident which took me out of the construction field permanently since I was no longer able to operate the heavy machinery. I had managed to lose my home, my family and, now, my occupation. Suicide seemed to be in order.

While contemplating ending it all, I remembered the words of my confirmation pastor. It was as though he were standing before me: "Son, when you snuff out your life, you will propel yourself into an eternity of damnation, for the choice of life and death is not yours to make." Desiring death and too frightened to take my life, I looked again at the whole situation. It was most evident that I was not capable of giving direction to my life. In utter desperation I cried out, "Jesus Christ, if you are real, make yourself real to me and I will turn my life over to you."

2

No bells rang - no cymbals clanged - no lights flashed - no great emotional outburst. Yet the reality of His presence was manifested. A deep inner peace filled my very being. It was the first peace I had ever known in my whole life. I knew for the first time that He was more than a doctrine, more than a learned principle. He is a living Person - the living God. And that peace has never left in spite of many trials and difficulties.

Life began to take on meaning as Jesus Christ took His rightful place in my life. Shortly after this, a position opened for me as an employment counselor with the State of Washington. While a deep inner peace had come with the decision to follow Jesus, the day-to-day living of life was still one of loneliness and little direction. The new career as an employment counselor occupied much of my day but always there was the night to face with its emptiness. Other than having a job, I still had little purpose and no goals.

Marriage to Shirley was a gift only the heavenly Father could give. Shirley brought needed stability into my life and God's blessings have showered upon me through her love. It is certainly true in life, as the scriptures teach, that a man is blessed by a woman sent by the heavenly Father.

However, those first years held great testing. I brought staggering debts into the marriage. After I was put on permanent status with the state agency and we were able to consolidate the indebtedness, the practice of drawing creditors' names from a hat came to an end. We were still at the poverty level but we were free of the indebtedness.

I was also a recovering alcoholic. In fact, Shirley had been warned "He is the town drunk and you will have nothing but problems." As we began taking our first spiritual steps together it might have seemed we were simply becoming religious. But what may have appeared as simply becoming religious from a worldly point of view was, in reality, the work of God. We began to see the presence of Christ in each other's life.

Those days were hectic and blessed as Shirley and I learned to walk, hand in hand, ever closer with our Lord. Many times we have reflected on those days of hardship and seen the marvelous grace of God in taking two people out of the stream of worldly futility and putting them together for His purposes. We were and still are close friends who share and confide our inner hurts and desires. We have never stopped talking one with the other. Days free from ministry responsibilities seldom see us doing house chores, we are too busy talking and sharing.

We are still lovers who desire always to please the other in all ways. What a blessing!

It soon became apparent that if I was to progress in my new career I would have to have more than a high school education. I enrolled in some junior college courses which, apparently, re-kindled in me the call to the ministry. I made inquiries and finally sought out counseling from my Lutheran pastor. I said little to Shirley at first but when I was assured that I would be accepted for training, I hesitantly asked for her thoughts. Her reply was, "If that is what you want, let's do it."

There was nothing in Shirley's past to prepare her for the role of a pastor's wife. Raised in a non-religious home and briefly involved in Christian Science, she had started an active church life because I had insisted that she become Lutheran if we married. My announcement did not particularly disturb her. If I wanted to make a career change at my age and that career was to be a pastor, she would support me. If she had known what the future held she might have had second thoughts. Her main thought at the time was it would be better than being the wife of an alcoholic as had been predicted when we married.

The first year at the seminary was difficult, to say the least. Shirley had never lived away from her family except for a brief time when we lived in Tacoma, Washington, and that was only a three hour drive. Now we were in Illinois, more than a half-continent from them. We knew no one and financially it was the worst since our first year of marriage. She had planned to work at her profession as a grocery checker but we found wages were less by nearly half. I tried to find work but did not until the second year. Our understanding of trusting God was stretched. Shirley made a commitment: "I'm going to get this man through school if I have to scrub floors to do it."

Eventually Shirley found a better job and I also found work that allowed me to continue my studies. During the second year I began to get preaching assignments to small town and rural churches. This provided us with the welcome opportunity for week-end trips. In looking back, we find this to have been a wonderful period of spiritual growth.

Upon graduation I was ordained a minister in the Lutheran Church-Missouri Synod and we accepted a call to South Dakota. Shirley's initiation into the life of the parsonage brought on strong feelings of inadequacy. Well-intentioned but unwise parishioners besieged her with requirements for music (for which she had never trained,)

4

teaching Sunday School and Vacation Bible School (which she felt temperamentally unsuited to do and leading women's groups (she had never before even prayed in public.) The one really bright spot was adopting John. As mother and wife she was adequate and with a new baby she was not expected to take a leading role in the church life.

My first move into spiritual renewal began with the acceptance of a call to serve a congregation in Southwest Idaho. I am sure events prior to that time are important, but the call to that church in 1968 is a pivotal event that led into the inner-healing/deliverance ministry. Little did I realize at that time just how deeply I would become involved in the move of the Holy Spirit taking place throughout the world.

Before my being called to it, this congregation had been involved in an in-depth evaluation of its goals and achievements. The study had shown them many areas of weakness as well as strengths. This was done before I accepted the call. With my installation as the new pastor, it was decided to correct or find ways to build up the congregation wherever weaknesses were found.

Shortly thereafter, the District introduced a parish renewal program. I was chosen to represent the circuit of which I and the congregation were members. My responsibility was to attend district meetings where I would be trained to implement the program in the circuit. The program was centered on the work of the Holy Spirit. It is interesting that the only congregation in that circuit which participated in the program was the one I served. The study resulted in the formation of working groups using the directives of the district program to study every facet of the congregation's spiritual life. These groups then set forth plans whereby the parish might come into spiritual renewal.

Out of this study and planning came an evening Bible study group which entered into intensive study of the person and work of the Holy Spirit. The class was well-attended, especially by many of the young adults. Many came from other denominations since interest was high at that time concerning the work of the Holy Spirit. Much was happening world-wide and people were seeking information which few denominational churches were willing to explore.

As the evening Bible class moved deeper into the study of the work of the Holy Spirit, I began to be recognized as a local leader in the spiritual renewal. This surprised me. Though I prayed with people to receive the gift of tongues and other gifts, I had not as yet received the gift of tongues. I was not opposed; to the contrary, I believed tongues to have strong, scriptural support. I had sought the Lord many times to ask Him for any gift He had to give to strengthen my ministry.

Some within the group began to seek the baptism with the Holy Spirit. Many received and many were speaking in other tongues. Requests came from those in attendance for more open worship services, more of the contemporary gospel music and more freedom in the liturgical services. To meet those requests, permission was granted by the Church Council to conduct a second morning worship service of a more contemporary nature.

With the new services and the on-going Bible study class, a new breath of spiritual life began to move through the congregation. Soon I was to find myself making soul-searching decisions concerning my own involvement in the spiritual renewal. A most crucial decision centered on my own synodical position as a Lutheran pastor. Could I truly enter into the spiritual renewal which I saw taking place and still remain a Lutheran minister?

I believed there was a need for honesty on my part. If I could not enter into the spiritual renewal without violating my vows as a Lutheran pastor, then I must make a choice between renewal and the Lutheran Church.

To resolve this, I decided to review the Lutheran Confessions which delineate the doctrines of the Lutheran theology. This would be the basis for my decision. I entered into this review as objectively as possible under the circumstances. It was my desire that the Confessions speak for themselves, not that I make them fit my wishes.

At that particular time, my convictions concerning spiritual renewal were not as fixed as they have since become. I truly believe that I was open to truth no matter what the result might be. That study of the Confessions left me with the conviction that I could enter fully into spiritual renewal as I saw it taking place throughout Christendom without violating the Lutheran Confessions.

However, it became most evident that I would be violating the traditions, the customs and the practices which had grown up around those Confessions. Many of those traditions and customs have taken to themselves an authority which I could not find clearly spelled out in the Confessions themselves. Now I felt I could remain within the Lutheran structure as a minister and teach the concepts of renewal without violating my ordination vows.

An Episcopalian couple approached me one evening at the Bible class to inquire if I knew of the approaching conference to be held in Minneapolis. This was the first Lutheran conference on the work of the Holy Spirit to be held in that city. When I indicated that I knew nothing about it, they briefly reviewed the information they had received from a friend. Then much to my amazement they offered to furnish the necessary funds that I might attend.

When asked why they wanted to do this, the response was that no other pastor in the area was willing to step into a leadership role in the spiritual renewal. Since the conference was for Lutherans, they felt I should attend.

Arriving at the conference, I saw the joy of the people as they sang in the Spirit, sharing together in worship and praise. I had never experienced such a sense of the presence of the Lord in a congregational setting. I realized that God was moving among His people in a way which was unfamiliar to me. I wanted to share in that worship and praise just as the others. This is not to say that I was unable to worship. It was impossible not to praise and worship the Lord in the midst of such an outpouring of the Spirit.

I returned to my hotel room after the first day of the conference determined to seek out the Lord on the matter of tongues. I knew that I had been baptized with the Holy Spirit. There was no question in my mind concerning this. Why then had I not received the gift of tongues? There was no reason apparent to me. It was most frustrating to stand in the presence of approximately 9,000 people singing and praising in the Spirit and not be able to participate. It was not a matter of trying. I tried everything. I made all kinds of sounds in the hope something would happen. But all that came were silly sounds - no exhilaration, no great stirring within, no touch of glory - just silly sounds.

I sought the Lord in prayer asking Him if I could have the gift. Surely He must know that if I was to be a leader in spiritual renewal, I should have the necessary gifts. I directed rather pointed questions to Him about the whole matter. Very early in the morning, after much wrestling with the Lord in prayer, I fell asleep. I had received no answer.

I attended many workshops on the work of the Holy Spirit but I was still unable to sing or pray in the Spirit. The second night there I set as a showdown with God. He did not set the showdown - I did. If I could not find answers to my questions or if I did not receive the gift of tongues, I would pack up my gear and catch the next plane for home. I would no longer serve in the spiritual renewal movement. I'm sure that did not worry the Lord for He can raise up men wherever they are needed. I have no illusions that I am indispensable in God's plan.

Very shortly after presenting my ultimatum to God, my mind suddenly went blank. It was only for a fraction of a second but every thought stopped momentarily. This was followed by a progression of Bible passages. First came the message from the Epistle to the Ephesians:

> ... and he gave some apostles and some prophets and some evangelists and some pastors and teachers, ... [Eph.4:11]

Next came the Lord's words to Ezekiel:

> Thus sayeth the Lord God unto these bones. Behold I will cause breath to enter into you and ye shall live. I will lay sinews upon you, and will bring up flesh upon you, and cover you with skin, and put breath in you, for ye shall know that I am the Lord. [Ezek.37:5,6]

And finally, Elijah's question to Elisha:

> ... Ask what I shall do for thee before I be taken away from thee. (And Elisha's reply:) I pray thee let a double portion of thy spirit be upon me. [II Kings 2:9]

With that scripture passage, there was again the momentary cessation of thought and my mind again returned to its normal functions.

I pondered for a considerable period of time over what had taken place. I knew God had spoken to me from out of His own word but I could not fathom what He was saying to me since I was seeking the gift of tongues. I sought the Lord for answers. I said, "Lord, I'm rather dense when you choose to speak to me. I do not always understand but I know You have spoken. What does it mean? Forgive me for not understanding."

Immediately, the previous thought patterns were repeated - my mind ceased to function momentarily and the following message was impressed on my mind:

> I am He who has raised you up out of the mire and the hell-pots of this world where I found you. I am the One

Who made it possible for you to attend the seminary and gave you the wisdom to finish the requirements. I am the One Who called you into the ministry in the Lutheran Church. I am the One Who sent you to the church that you now serve. It was not your choice but Mine. I am the One that will remove you from that call only when I choose. It was not your choice or the choice of men but Mine where you are called to serve.

I have called you to serve in the great thing I am doing in My Church throughout the world. You are now serving a church which is filled with dry bones but those bones shall rise up and walk again. They shall receive life and they shall know that I am the Lord. You have already received a double measure of the Spirit who motivated and empowered Elijah, Elisha, and all those who serve according to My call. You do not now need the gift of tongues to serve Me wherein I have called you. Worship Me with the gifts you now possess.

Now I knew why. Now I could return to the conference knowing that I was in God's will, able to worship without any reservation though I did not yet possess the gift of tongues. I wonder how many feel some doubt in the spiritual renewal because they do not yet possess the gift of tongues? How many question or even feel guilt because of this apparent lack and the insistence on the part of some that tongues is absolutely necessary? Praise God, He removed all that for me.

I returned to the conference with great joy, knowing that the Lord had His plan and I fit somewhere in that plan. I worshipped Him with freedom and with joy. The balance of the time which I served that congregation, I never received the gift of tongues even though I prayed for others to receive and they did. Time has allowed me to see why the gift was delayed. Had I received the gift, the lay leadership would have demanded my immediate removal. The Lord withheld the gift in order to draw together the dry bones which would one day rise up and walk out of that congregation.

It is most interesting how little we grasp of what the Lord says to us. About one year after my dismissal from that congregation and the formation of the new one, I was pondering that portion of His message concerning the dry bones. I thought: "How are those dry bones going to walk now that I have been removed from the congregation? They have now moved into a more rigid, traditional stance than before." Immediately, the following message was impressed upon my mind: "Why is it that you have so much difficulty seeing and understanding my works? Where do you think the present congregation you are serving came from? Did not the dry bones rise up and walk just as I said they would? Did not they receive life and rise up and walk out of that place of unrest?" I praised the Lord, for then I knew the words spoken in Minneapolis had been fulfilled.

Our arrival at the parsonage in Idaho had been a rather strange experience for Shirley and me. Both of us felt very depressed during the first visit. Even before our furniture arrived I was required to go to a district meeting, leaving Shirley in a cold, nearly vacant house in a strange town. She described the house as unhappy and depressed. I experienced a strong impression that I should resign the call and present myself for a call to another place. It was set aside by rationalizing that I was probably just feeling the lingering sorrow associated with leaving the previous congregation. It is most difficult to explain what we felt other than to say the building had an atmosphere of unrest and uneasiness.

We were not there long before unusual things were happening. Shirley reports that she would be upstairs, hear a door open, footsteps walk across a room but when she went down no one would be there. The laundry facilities were in the basement. While working there she would hear footsteps across the upper floor. Knowing I was gone but supposing I had forgotten something and returned, she would come upstairs to find, again, no one there.

As time passed, we began to notice other rather strange events occurring. Two Siamese cats came with us from the home in South Dakota. Since they were housebroken, they spent a great deal of time in the house. On several occasions, both became very frightened and crawled to the door. Once the door was opened they would bolt out and run away from the house. We might have passed these occurrences off, had they not also occurred when the weather was inclement and we knew that they would rather be indoors than outdoors. Something truly had frightened them. Whatever it was, it was not visible to us nor were we able to detect a physical cause.

There were other occasions when the cats would awake from a sound sleep, leap into the air, tails completely fluffed and the hair raised on their back. They would streak for the door and when outside run away from the house. Again, there was no visible or physical cause for such action. Neither of the cats had ever acted in this manner before. Something was striking fear into those animals. Shirley and I pondered

10

what could be taking place for it defied rational explanation.

A later series of events staggered our minds for we were, again, unable to explain them. A family in the congregation had given us a plaque which we had placed on our dining room wall. A nail was driven into a wall stud at an upward angle. In order to remove the plaque, one needed to lift it up directly from the nail. One day as we were sitting at the kitchen table, the plaque suddenly fell from the wall. We ran in to see what had fallen and saw the plaque lying on the floor about three feet out. I looked at the wall - the nail was firmly in place. I checked the windows; all were closed so a draft could not be responsible. There had been no sonic booms or other natural causes. Somehow, some way, that plaque had raised from the nail and fallen to the floor about three feet from the wall. Shirley and I looked at one another not daring to say what each of us was thinking.

A short time after this, Shirley and I were seated in our living room when another strange event occurred. A newspaper had been left lying on the dining room table, neatly folded (a strong habit of mine.) Suddenly we heard the paper fall to the floor. Our first thought was that our toddler son, John, had pulled it down. Then we remembered he had been put to bed; it was not possible that he had moved the paper. I went into the dining room. The paper was lying on the floor two to three feet from the table - neatly folded. Not one page was out of order. It lay as though someone had picked it up and placed it on the floor. Shirley and I shook our heads in disbelief.

Perhaps the most perplexing occurrence involved two bags of cat litter. Shirley had purchased the litter and placed them on the floor next to the furnace in the basement. After much delay on my part and insistence on her part I decided to change the litter box. No bags of litter were to be found. We searched the basement without success. Finally, I bought two more bags and filled the litter box. The next morning I opened the basement door to let the cats out, looked down the stairs and there stood the two bags of litter next to the furnace. It defied explanation.

These and many other strange events continued for four years. Shirley began to dread being in the house alone and for a considerable period of time begged me to never be gone overnight. I chided her about it for she had never expressed such fear before. I reminded her that the property was well-lighted and there was little chance of anyone breaking in. Finally, she said, "I know you'll think I'm crazy or something, but I have no fear of what is outside of the house. I have no fear of someone forcing their way in. I'm afraid of the house and what is in it."

At that moment, I realized Shirley was sensing and believing that something other than normal, explainable occurrences were happening. We sat down and began to compare notes back to the time we first visited the parsonage. There was definitely something wrong in that house or else we were both victims of over-active imaginations. I made it a point to avoid overnight meetings, if possible. I was reprimanded several times for missing district meetings but I could not share the problem with my fellow Lutheran pastors since I felt they would not have understood.

There were occurrences which took place in the church which also left questions in my mind. Approximately one month after my arrival in the parish, I was working in the church office. There was a coat hook on a door leading into the sanctuary upon which an empty coat hanger hung. While working on a study paper, I heard a strange sound and looked up to see the coat hanger swinging back and forth. I was fascinated by the fact it did not lose momentum, but to the contrary, it swung back and forth the same distance for a considerable period of time.

My first thought was of an earthquake. A quick glance at the hanging light in the office dispensed that thought for it stood perfectly still. Perhaps a draft of air was the cause. I looked to see if the outside door might be open, but it was closed. A quick check of the sanctuary confirmed there had been no earthquake for the hanging chandeliers stood perfectly still. But something had moved that coat hanger and was continuing to move it.

Perhaps the strangest and most chilling incident took place shortly before I was forced to leave the pastorate. It occurred during an evening Bible study class. That class was made up of a number of young adults with little children. Two teen-aged girls watched over the children while the parents attended the class. A partition separated the class from the area in the basement where the children played. It was our custom to close the class with round-table prayer, giving each person an opportunity to pray. As the final person finished, the door burst open and the children and the two teen-aged girls rushed into the room. Their eyes and faces reflected fear. Most of the children ran and clutched their parents tightly. Something was definitely wrong. When I questioned the older of the girls she said, "Please, come into the other room with me."

She led me into a smaller room just off the basement where the children often played. I followed her into that room whereupon she closed the door and turned off the light. Turning to me, she said, "What do you see?" "Nothing," I replied. However, at that moment I experienced a strong feeling of coldness and oppression. "Look at the window.

What do you see there?" she asked.

I was surprised, for I could not see through the window. This startled me since I should have been able to see shrubs and the parsonage in the illumination of the yard light. But the window was completely dark as though covered with something. I assumed the yard light was burned out. I turned the room light on and asked what was going on. She replied, "What did you see in the window?" "Nothing. What was I supposed to see?" She replied quite calmly, "The face of Satan."

I looked at the window again and to my surprise, I could see the shrubs and parsonage quite clearly. A look of shock and disbelief must have been on my face, for she blurted out, "It was there. It was there. All the kids saw it and they began to cry." She continued, "One of the younger children was asleep on a bench. He woke up screaming and pointing at the window. That is when we saw the face of Satan."

She said they rushed the children out into the main basement and waited for us to finish the class. Neither of the teen-agers were prone to exaggerate or given to over-active imaginations. I was convinced they had seen something.

The adults were gathered together and told what had happened. We prayed together for wisdom and for protection. As the members left, I asked one man to stay for a short period of time. He was not a member of the congregation but I had been told he was a man who had knowledge concerning the areas of supernatural happenings. I sought his advice in this matter. He said we should go through the whole building and rid it of any demonic forces which might be present.

I immediately asked, "Do you have the knowledge and experience to cleanse the building?" He replied he had no firsthand experience but had done considerable reading about cleansing houses of unclean spirits. I knew the events of this night would not be accepted graciously by the already perturbed lay leadership of the congregation, but I requested that he get on with it so we would not have these kinds of things going on in the church.

So it was that the four of us (our sons, John and Tim, were with me because Shirley was working in a convenience store) set out on a tour of the building to cleanse it of unclean spirits. The man pleaded the blood of Jesus Christ upon the doorjambs, window frames, walls, floors and so forth in every room of the building and every unclean spirit was commanded to leave the rooms. Every closet and storage area was dealt with in the same manner.

After each part of the building had been dealt with, the man announced the building was now free of all evil forces. I must confess I felt no manifestations of unclean spirits being present or leaving. I could only hope what he said was true. Bidding the man God's blessing, the boys and I returned to the parsonage. I tucked the boys in immediately, as they were very young and utterly exhausted.

I sat down to ponder all that had occurred. Could all this have really happened? And if it were real, why did it happen to me? It seemed I had enough problems without the Lord allowing this to occur on top of it all. The longer I sat there and pondered, the more uneasy I became. It seemed as if the whole house was alive or at least there was a tremendous power being manifested which I could not explain.

I was very concerned for John and Tim as both had been subject to walking in their sleep. On several occasions John had slipped out of bed in the middle of the night, taking Tim by the hand and leading him downstairs and out of the house. When we questioned John as to why he led his brother out of the house, he would reply, "I had to get him out. I had to get him out."

I decided to clear up the supper dishes. Perhaps this would get my mind off the events of the evening and the feelings I was experiencing. It was also possible the Lord might grant some insight into the whole situation. Suddenly, I heard a spine-chilling scream from the upstairs bedroom. I bounded up the stairs in one or two strides and ran into the boys' bedroom. John was standing over Tim's crib screaming for him to wake up and to get up. I picked John up. His eyes were filled with fear. "What is the matter," I asked. "Why are you screaming?" He continued to scream, "We've got to get out of the house. We've got to get out of the house."

I finally quieted him down and held him close until the fear subsided. He agreed it would be all right if he and Tim went to sleep in Mom and Dad's bed. I tucked them in, prayed for them, and sat with them until they fell asleep. I decided then that this was enough; something was dreadfully wrong in that house. It was not a physical problem nor was I having an emotional problem. This was a spiritual problem and it needed to be dealt with on a spiritual basis.

I prayed, seeking the Lord's guidance. The conviction came that I should rid that home of every unclean spirit which had invaded it and was tormenting us, especially John and Tim. I was not convinced that what the man had done in the church had been effective. Somehow I could not see how pleading the blood on the doorjambs, window frames, etc., would free the building of evil spirits. This is not to say I reject this means, but that night I was not convinced.

I went first into the bedroom where I had put the boys. I made the sign of the cross in the air and, in a calm but as authoritarian voice as I could muster, commanded every unclean spirit in that room to depart in the name and the blood of the Lord Jesus Christ. To my amazement, all feelings of oppression and heaviness in the room disappeared. I could not believe what I was experiencing. A sudden peace came into the room. All was at rest. I praised God and thanked Him for what had happened.

I stepped out into the hall to go to the next room. It was like stepping into an area filled with oppression and awesome, depressing power. Again, I made the sign of the cross and commanded all unclean spirits out. The result was the same. The heaviness and oppression vanished immediately. Peace and rest came into that hallway. Again, I praised God and proceeded throughout the whole house in the same manner.

I returned to our bedroom to check the boys. They were sound asleep with no indications of fear or any other problems. Now was time to relax and search the Scriptures to find God's answers to all that had occurred. After about an hour-and-a-half, Shirley returned from work. As she came through the door, she stopped, looked at me and said, "What have you been doing?" "Nothing," I replied. She looked at me with that look she gets when she knows I'm not telling all of the truth and said, "Well, I know you've done something. Please tell me what it is."

I shared with her all that had happened that night including the casting out of the unclean spirits in the home. She smiled and said, "This is the first time I've ever come into this house and felt that it was at rest and peace. Now I believe I can come to love living in this home." (Unfortunately, we were not to live in that home much longer, for the forces were being gathered to drive us out of that pastorate.)

The next day I went over to the church facility early in the morning and went through every part of the building in the same manner as I had in the parsonage. Never again would I have to minster there with manifestations of evil spirits in that building other than those manifested in the actions of men.

15

In the parsonage there were no more plaques falling from walls nor papers from the table; cats no longer leaped into the air terrified. Shirley no longer feared when I would leave for overnight meetings. Now the house was at peace and at rest. It was a beautiful home in which to live. John and Tim settled down and the midnight excursions from the bedroom to the outdoors came to an end. There was a wondrous peace which came upon the family. My only regret is the same peace did not come upon the whole congregation but too much had happened and too much had been initiated by that time.

The lay leadership of the congregation reacted to these events much as one might have predicted. As the world would say: "All hell broke loose."

"Now that pastor's brought Satan right into the church, who knows what he will do next." "That is exactly what happens when they begin to get away from true doctrine."

These are but a few of the things which were said. Had it not been so tragic, it would have been humorous for many who spoke those words did not even believe Satan exists. Now it was imperative to get rid of the pastor. The congregation would be the laughing stock of the community. It would be the home of Satan as long as this pastor remained. But how do you get rid of a minister who has brought Satan into the church? How do you go about it without acknowledging Satan has been in the church?

The events which followed were most distressing. I hesitate to credit their planning to any human source for they were so devilish in nature. A smear campaign began against Shirley and me. It had but one goal: total character assassination and the destruction of the ministry to which I was called.

The gossip mills ground out the stories: I was supposedly involved in adultery with various women; Shirley was said to be acting immorally with the manager of the store where she worked; drunkenness and total degradation were alleged. To this very day, there are ministers in that area, who have never met me, yet speak of me as an immoral reprobate.

There is much more that could be cited but it would only serve the purposes of Satan. Let it suffice to say that Satan must have rejoiced with glee as his purposes were fulfilled. Little did my family and I realize how devastating the fury of Satan could be until experienced at a personal level. Now we had seen it face to face.

16

The first pastorate in Idaho had proved to be very difficult and a most trying experience. There's little doubt that my involvement in the spiritual renewal was a devastating blow to the staid, tradition-bound and conservative lay leadership of that congregation. Many felt threatened by their pastor's willingness to examine the renewal and to open himself to whatever the Holy Spirit might offer. There were other factors which also contributed to the difficulties and also served to move me deeper into the spiritual renewal.

The congregation was beset, as many are, with counter-flowing internal power structures. Satan always welcomes these situations as opportunities for his destructive work. These counter-flowing forces within the congregational structure caused a form of strife which often defied comprehension. A younger element in the congregation desired more voice in the affairs at hand but were thwarted by the older conservative leadership. The prevailing philosophy seemed to be age always begets wisdom and without age youth was without the necessary wisdom for leadership. I found myself walking a tightrope between the two factions.

Another group of people found its calling centered in the affairs of the Christian Day School operated by the congregation. The demands of that school were a strain upon the financial resources of the congregation. Still another group found its calling centered in the church facilities and worship needs. Here again, I walked a very taut tightrope between these emotionally charged groups. To support any one group was to immediately incur the displeasure of the others. The balance of the congregation fluctuated between the demands of the other groups.

Beneath the surface were hidden forces which were able to manipulate situations in such a way as to turn them into utter chaos. Problems arose which defied normal pastor-congregational relationships. Decisions reached in council and voter meetings would suddenly be twisted and turned into chaos causing me to cry out in frustration, "What in the world has happened? How have we arrived at this point? When was that said?" Time after time solutions to problems were reached and arrangements made only to see them shattered and destroyed within hours or days. Then would follow accusations and charges laying blame and responsibility.

Perhaps the most devastating and heart-rending times were those created by the gossip mills. In David Wilkerson's prophecy, he speaks of Satan's attacks upon men willing to follow the call of God in the spiritual renewal. He speaks of false charges of adultery, immorality,

17

drunkenness, false teachings and many others. Shirley and I were to hear all of them. It is unbelievable what Satan can plant in the minds of idle gossipers and those dedicated to their own causes. For the first time in my life I was seeing spiritual warfare firsthand but as yet I was unable to see clearly the hand of Satan working through men and women. I saw only men and women intent upon destroying my character and the ministry to which I was called. I reacted accordingly, adding fuel to the fires of strife and bitterness, wreaking havoc for all concerned.

The point of no return had been reached. The internal power struggles within the congregation, my involvement with the spiritual renewal, the gossip and the determined efforts of the lay leadership culminated in a plan to bring about my resignation. Returning from a vacation, I was surprised to learn a series of meetings had been held under the guidance of the District Synodical office. A letter demanding my resignation had been drafted with a deadline set for complying. Failure to comply would result in a congregational meeting where charges would be brought and my removal from pulpit duty would be assured. I decided, wise or unwise, not to tender my resignation. To resign would be an admission of guilt to all the charges which had been made, including vicious character assassinations.

The meeting was set and the night in which the meeting was held found me in a hospital bed. The charges were presented which included such things as pastoral neglect, no compassion for people, drunkenness, adultery (by both Shirley and I) and the other rumors ground out by the gossip mills. No response was allowed by those seeking my defense. The charges were made, the vote was taken and my dismissal resulted. Not one charge was ever substantiated. Even now, more than a decade later, the gossip mills still continue to do their job. Not one accusation of heresy, unbiblical teaching or violation of Lutheran doctrine was raised. One man later said "What we did was not right, but it was expedient that it be done." It was not the spiritual renewal which caused the mock trial - it was the work of men dedicated to my removal.

As a result of that congregational action thirty-five frustrated families decided that night to form a new congregation. This included elders and other leaders. They asked me to serve them as pastor. My first reaction was to say "No!" and to leave the area. However, I felt a responsibility to those calling me for they had supported me through the trials and turmoil of those hectic days. Furthermore, they had caught something of the vision of spiritual renewal.

In the midst of this great trial God had a special blessing waiting

18

for me. What had put me in the hospital was a ruptured appendix and shortly after the meeting my condition worsened. Peritonitis had developed. The infection accompanying that affliction spread, closing the bile duct. Death was stalking me as poison flowed through my body. Each day I sank lower and lower but I could not accept death as being God's will.

I finally decided to call the leaders of the new congregation to anoint me with oil and pray a prayer for healing. As I lay there considering placing a call to the men, God, our heavenly Father, intervened. He spoke gently but firmly: "No, you shall not call the men of the congregation. This is a matter between you and Me. You will be healed when you submit yourself to Me."

I was devastated. Surely I was in submission to His will. Had I not just been voted out of a pulpit because I took a stand for what I believed He asked of me? Had I not accepted a leadership role to bring spiritual renewal into the Lutheran Church? Was I not willing to go wherever He asked me to serve Him? Had I not opened myself to any and every gift which the Holy Spirit might offer?

I had gone through that surgery with complete trust in His providential care. Where had I failed to submit? I looked back to see where I might have failed Him. I set out everything and anything which might stand between myself and the heavenly Father. Every possible sin was recalled and confessed; yet no answer came. There was only that silence of all silences which comes when the Lord does not seem to communicate. I pleaded for some clue, some reason, some indication of what it was that stood between us, but the silence continued.

In desperation, I cried out: "God, I do not know what stands between us. I do not know where I have failed to submit myself to Your will. But I do know that if You choose to reach down now and to snuff out my life, I cannot stop you. I have no power over you. I am completely under your control. If it is Your will that I should die, let it be. I do not know what you are asking of me, but if You want me to say 'I submit,' then, Father - I submit."

Immediately I felt peace within my soul and I knew, at that very moment, I would be healed. The healing began and strength flowed in each new day. It was a considerable period of time before my strength returned. (It is interesting that the critical healing period was of the same duration as the number of days of decline.) I still do not know what stood between us. I can only conclude that the Lord was calling for a complete submission upon my part in order for me to enter into the inner healing/ deliverance ministry.

Upon my release from the hospital I took up my pastoral duties with the new congregation. I saw a whole new ministry opening up before me. I was able to see that the reality of spiritual renewal was possible. Pastor and people set out to open themselves to the Holy Spirit's leading with the hope and prayer that a truly charismatic congregation might emerge. We even dared to hope it could occur within the setting of the Lutheran Church. The congregation applied for and received membership in the same synod from which originally it had come.

The congregation moved slowly into New Testament concepts. However, it was not always a smooth transition. Zealous Pentecostals, who came into the congregation, chaffed under the Lutheran traditionalism which persisted. The remaining Lutherans resisted the pentecostalism which was rearing its head. We were caught on the horns of a dilemma: too Pentecostal for the Lutherans and too Lutheran for the Pentecostals.

It was amusing, yet tragic, to see how bound one can become by liturgical ties. I say this for I still love and respect liturgical forms of worship. They come out of a heritage which should not be cast away and forgotten. The most traditional liturgical worship service can still bring one to a deep worship of God. Unfortunately, it has lost its worship value because people have lost the understanding of the liturgy and of its purpose. For some the liturgy is but an exercise in rote memory.

This bondage was also evident in the congregational singing. As we began to sing the Pentecostal style songs of praise, it became most evident that people could not sing at the rapid pace set by many of the tunes. However, after a period of time, this too, was overcome and the congregation slowly moved into a free and open worship service. Praise became more spontaneous and less liturgical.

A Wednesday evening service was added. It began as an instructive service but soon became a prayer, praise and worship service. It resulted in consternation for many. Some asked, "How fanatical is the Pastor going to get? Soon he will have us in church every night of the week." While it was hoped that the mid-week service would lead into a deeper, more meaningful growth in worship, unrest proved to be present. Some sought a return to the security of the liturgy and a clergy-dominated type of service. Yet another group sought a rapid move into a more Pentecostal type of service.

Disagreements over styles of worship and order of service were mild compared to some of the other strife-engendering problems that came to this congregation. Shortly after word got around that a charismatic Lutheran congregation had been established, a group began to attend apparently hoping to plant their pet doctrine. They believed that the proof of salvation was speaking in tongues. Therefore, if one did not yet speak in tongues it was questionable that he was saved. Every effort to bring these teachings to the test of Holy Scripture was twisted and perverted until chaos ruled supreme.

Another source of strife found root in plans to lodge a protest against the former congregation because of the unproved (and unfounded) charges they had brought concerning Shirley and me. Now the leadership of the new congregation decided to drop the protest. This infuriated some who wanted the other congregation punished. When these had no outward foes to battle they turned in upon the local congregation.

In an attempt to deal with these problems, the leadership decided to introduce teachings by a well-known California minister that centers on the concept of "body ministry." In this teaching the people are to seek out one another for prayer and counseling rather than always going to a professional clergy. It also brings people to face the Lord's requirements for the life of sanctification. This caused many to feel that the Law was being emphasized. They could not, apparently, see the difference between "should" and "must." Soon there arose the accusation that the preacher was too heavy on the Law and short on the Gospel.

Turmoil again swirled about me. Tension was building as I sought every means possible to hold all the factions together yet allow the Holy Spirit freedom. Many times I sought the Lord, pleading that He allow me to move into another ministry or to another congregation if I was the cause of the unrest in this congregation. Each time it seemed the answer was to remain and serve in this call.

Shortly after the new congregation had begun holding services in a rural community hall, a young man suggested I attend a conference with him in Sunburst, Montana. He implied to me that the Lord had directed him to extend an invitation to me. At first, I was very hesitant to commit myself. I could think of no valid reason for my attendance. I prayed about the matter and soon came under the conviction that I should attend.

I was very puzzled by this because everything he shared concerning the conference troubled me. From his description, it sounded like a "far-out" conference with emotionally oriented meetings. Finally, I did agree to go but only because some inner drive was motivating me.

I was somewhat taken aback by the openness and sincerity of the people involved, though it was just as emotional as I had suspected it would be. I was not accustomed to Christians embracing one another and speaking of love one for another. Likewise, I was not prepared to hear Christians remind me that God loved me and we should praise the Lord together. This had never happened to me in the Lutheran Church since the formal services do not allow for this type of activity. Furthermore, such emotional outbursts would be frowned upon in a Lutheran church.

But in these people gathered in Sunburst, I sensed the work of the Holy Spirit in a way I had not found in many churches. There was a spirit of peace and joy and love that was very contagious. Soon I, too, began to move under the motivating power of the Spirit which prevailed throughout the conference. It must be said that I was in theological disagreement with a great deal of what was being taught. Yet I could not escape the reality that God was using the conference for His own purpose in my life. Furthermore, I could not deny there was a bond of unity which united me to these people in spite of our theological differences.

I knew only God could bring that bond. Harold Bredesen was one of the speakers. On the evening he was to speak, he arose and announced the Lord was moving him to abandon his prepared presentation. He felt there were some present who had experienced problems with the gift of tongues or were seeking the gift. In the light of this, he began to share the reality of tongues. As he spoke, I felt a stirring and a longing which had not surfaced since the conference in Minneapolis. Once again, the desire for the gift rose within me.

When the invitation came, I was one of the first forward. As I knelt, praying as instructed, Harold came to me and asked what my problem might be. I told him how God had spoken to me in Minneapolis and shared that I believed now was the time for me to receive the gift.

He replied, "And why don't you just receive and speak?" I explained that I had tried, even making strange sounds, but I was convinced I was just babbling words I made up. He told me to do whatever I had been doing. Hearing my efforts, he touched my shoulder in a comforting way and said, "Brother, you have received the gift. Now go and glorify the Lord with it."

22

I continued, not convinced it was of the Lord but willing to accept if it was. Finally, I arose and sought out a man I had come to trust very much since arriving at the conference. I shared all which had just happened and asked him to step out where it was quiet so he could hear what I was babbling.

We stepped out of the meeting to a quiet place. He said I should pray in my language and he would pray in his. I responded that I did not have a new prayer language. He said, "Well, do whatever it was you were doing in there." He began to praise God in his prayer language and I hesitantly began to speak as I had inside the building. After a moment, he embraced me and with tears in his eyes, said, "Brother, you have it - you have it! Praise God!"

For a long period of time I wondered why there had been no emotional outburst, no great anointing, nothing spectacular. Of course, I had not taken into consideration the fact I'd already been baptized with the Spirit before attending the conference in Sunburst.

That same evening as I knelt to pray in the meeting, a young man from Puerto Rico came to me saying that the Lord had instructed him to share a message with me. The message said that I was to receive the gift of knowledge. The gift was to enhance the counseling I would be called into enabling me, in some cases, to know a person's problems before they were shared. I had never seen the man before nor did he know me prior to this meeting. Since that time, I have experienced the use and reality of the gift of knowledge just as he said I would. It is not a gift which manifests at all times but is surely cherished when it does function, especially in counseling sessions.

One could hardly expect much more to happen at the conference, but then the Lord does not always function according to our expectations. Robert Ewing, a dear brother, was to speak but asked another to take his place because God had another task for him that morning. The meeting had hardly begun when Harold Bredesen came and asked if I would leave the meeting to speak with him. I was somewhat surprised when Robert Ewing also arose to leave the meeting with us. I was also somewhat disturbed because I thought Robert was pushing himself into a private discussion. I was even more perturbed when we were joined by a former Mennonite minister and a young man from my own congregation who had come to the conference with me.

Little did I know what the next hour would hold. We proceeded to the host pastor's house. Harold Bredesen opened the conversation with several questions concerning the internal problems which were then raging within the Lutheran Synod which I served. In the midst of the conversation, the phone rang. It was an important call for Pastor Bredesen. He returned from the call to announce that he must leave immediately.

Robert Ewing then engaged me in idle conversation for a few moments. We had never met before this conference and he had never been to Idaho. He looked at his watch and said, "Exactly seven days ago to the minute God spoke to me and said I would meet two men from Idaho. This is the message He commissioned me to give to that one He directed me to place my hand upon his head." At this point Robert reached out, placed his hand upon my head, and spoke these words:

> This is the vessel I have chosen for that thing which I shall do. You have come forth through great trial and tribulation because you have heeded My call to stand firm. You have been ostracized and continue to be ridiculed by your fellow clergymen, by your synod, and by your community. I know your trials, how you have been falsely accused, but you are very dear to Me. I will use you in a mighty way if you will but follow Me.

The message continued, citing how the new congregation had come out of a time of travail and rejection. It also recounted a message that God had given to me concerning the congregation. Surely this was from God for Robert had no way of knowing the information he was speaking. Before coming to the conference, I had been in deep soul-searching concerning a proposed trip to Denmark. I was not sure if the trip was a divine call or one of my own desires. Then from Robert came these words:

> You will leave the present body of members you now serve in order to travel across the ocean for a short period of time. You will return to be given further training and then you will cross the ocean once again and for a longer period of time. When you return I will establish a body out of which will flow men and women unto all the parts of the world. In all of this, I will change your heart and restructure your mind.

At the evening service, in the midst of his sermon, the speaker stopped and spoke words that caused me to nearly leap out of my chair:

I do not know why I am to share this message tonight for it runs counter to my own convictions. I have never approved of quickie overseas missionary trips where someone flies in for a short stay and then departs. I believe a person is to commit himself to an extended period of time to truly be used of the Lord. But the Lord is saying that there is a person or persons here tonight whom He is calling to a short visit to a foreign land. All doubt concerning the call is to be set aside and the call answered.

Never before had I experienced anything like this. The conference at Sunburst proved to be a pivotal point in my ministry. I do not say this on the basis of the prophecies which were given for it is most dangerous to establish a ministry on prophecy alone. The conference was instrumental in breaking down my resistance to new concepts I could not readily fit into my spiritual heritage. Since that day I have been reluctant to reject a concept new to me until such time as biblical research indicates rejection is in order. The conference also proved to be a meeting point between God and myself. When I accepted the call of God into the present ministry of healing for spirit, soul and body, the call was accepted regardless of what it might cost me.

I called Shirley to report how the Lord had opened tongues to me, expecting she would rejoice with me. To my dismay, her reaction was one of great coldness. I should have expected this considering all she had been subjected to because of the turmoil between the leadership of the previous congregation and myself. In a vulnerable position as a grocery checker in a local store, daily she faced the innuendos, cutting remarks and hostility by members of that congregation but was required to smile and be pleasant.

When I called from Sunburst to report I had spoken in tongues, it was the last straw. Crushed and angry she felt betrayed by God and her husband. As I had become more involved in the Spiritual Renewal, Shirley began to feel left behind. As spiritual renewal opened for me, it seemed as though everything worked against Shirley. Two adopted boys, a home to keep up, a position as a grocery checker and the duties of a minister's wife seemed to rob her of the things I was experiencing in the renewal.

I was off to meetings in Minnesota, Michigan and Montana. Shirley remained at home caring for the children, working at the stores (especially hard after the dismissal from one church and the formation of the second) and trying to deal with sarcastic questions about what her husband was up to **now!** It must have been devastating to look at those years of sacrifice to enter the ministry and then see the carnage that rejection and bitterness had caused toward that ministry. Now her final defense was gone: Frank speaks in tongues - his fall was complete, so the leadership of the previous congregation would say.

I returned home with mixed emotions. On the one hand, I was overjoyed with all that had occurred; on the other, I knew Shirley was hurt and depressed over what I had shared with her concerning the conference. We had always been very close in all of our spiritual experiences. If one received something from the Lord, the other, in most cases, was sure to receive shortly thereafter. However, in the past few months it had seemed much was happening to me and she was being passed by.

Now it came to mind that perhaps, in some way, I had betrayed her. Could it be God was cheating her out of the gifts I was receiving? She became very angry at God feeling He had come between us. Later she told me: "If you had been guilty of an affair with another woman, I could have handled it. But how do you handle the jealousy which arises when it seems that God has moved between you and your husband?"

She carried these feelings for about a year even though she was going through the motions of being a Spirit-filled pastor's wife. In desperation one morning, she cried out to God: "What do I have to do to be acceptable to You?" God's reply was succinct and to the heart: "All you have to do is love Me." This was the beginning of the way out for her. God had spoken to her personally and she could depend on His love.

Shirley still had a long period of struggle to come to know and accept the love of others. In fact, it was not until she experienced a personal and unique deliverance from a spirit of rejection (among others) that she was to know complete freedom. During this time Shirley began to take an increasingly active part in the ministry and the gifts of the Spirit, especially discerning of spirits, were evident in her ministry. She has a tremendous and valuable witness to share with wives and husbands whose spouses are being drawn into spiritual renewal. Many people have come to see how the enemy uses this jealousy toward God to destroy family relationships in order to also destroy ministries. The testing was severe but the witness is most valuable.

One of the benefits of attending the first Lutheran Conference on the Work of the Holy Spirit was an invitation to participate in a Lutheran

Leaders' Conference at Ann Arbor, Michigan. There I met Dr. Michael Harry, a gynecologist from Denmark.

Dr. Harry, by the leading of the Holy Spirit, had worked with the pastors of the Lutheran State Churches of Denmark and Norway to become involved in spiritual renewal. In 1973, four or five pastors were willing to acknowledge publicly that they were involved in spiritual renewal and had received the baptism with the Holy Spirit. Dr. Harry came to the conference in Ann Arbor to plead with Spirit-filled Lutheran pastors to come to Scandinavia and share with the pastors there.

As I sat in that meeting listening to his plea, the Lord's call to go engulfed my whole being. I was shocked at the intensity of the experience. I remembered my first realization, as a youth, that God was calling me to the ministry. This call was much more powerful in nature. I set it aside immediately as an emotional response to the plea.

Several months passed by while I wrestled with two contradictory thoughts. First was the thought that self-glory and the excitement of travel to a foreign country was a motivating factor. The second centered in the reality of a call by God to go to Scandinavia for service in His kingdom. The prophecy spoken in Sunburst, Montana, brought confirmation that the call was of God.

Three visits to Scandinavia resulted from that meeting in Ann Arbor. The first dealt with the baptism of the Holy Spirit; the second looked at the general ministry of healing; and the third shared the insights into the inner healing/deliverance ministry.

The first trip, in February, 1973, brought me to Roskilde, Denmark, where the leaders of the renewal movement in Denmark had invited me to attend the conference on the work of the Holy Spirit. There I was invited to a meeting of the pastors giving them opportunity to size me up. This would allow the pastors the opportunity to invite me into their respective parishes. The conference drew pastors involved in renewal, interested in renewal, skeptical of renewal and the just plain curious.

The result was a twenty-one day teaching and preaching tour, including one week in Norway. I lived in the homes of pastors, speaking and sharing with those who had some interest in renewal. The majority of the pastors really desired to see firsthand what a Spirit-filled Lutheran pastor from America looked like. Some, with whom I shared, later became involved in the spiritual renewal. It should be noted there was a handful of faithful ministers of God throughout Scandinavia who had spent several years working to bring renewal to the Lutheran Church. My sharing, in many cases, built upon the work they had done.

The tour through the cities and hamlets of Denmark was a period of testing. I had been unable to prepare a comprehensive format of material to be shared before leaving America. I had sincerely tried but it seemed the Lord overruled every effort. I now understand why. I was being taught in the areas of submission and dependence upon the Lord. A passage of scripture became a living reality: "But when they deliver you up, take no thought how or what ye shall speak: for it shall be given you in that same hour what ye shall speak. For it is not ye that speak, but the Spirit of your Father which speaketh in you." [Mt.10:19,20]

Day by day I traveled through that land, never knowing to whom I would be speaking. It might be a handful of people or a whole congregation. I addressed young people in confirmation classes, groups of women, mixed groups of men and women, and gatherings of ministers and teachers. On several occasions, I was met at railway stations, told that I was to speak in a few minutes, and whisked away.

Upon arriving at an assembly, I would learn the nature of the gathering. I would pray for guidance by the Holy Spirit and start up the aisle to the speaker's platform. Many times a Bible passage would come to my mind and upon reaching the platform the message the Lord desired to share would begin to form in my mind. More than once the host would comment: "That was just what we needed to hear. Thank you so much." The Lord knew what He wanted said and what He wanted done. My role was to be in submission and allow the message to come from my lips. What a learning experience for this headstrong preacher.

A request came from Bergen, Norway, asking that I come to that city. Arrangements were made and I flew into a rugged and beautiful country. It was my privilege to speak before a city-wide meeting of the Full Gospel Business Men in Bergen. It was an evening meeting and included wives and guests. Before the meeting, I again wrestled with the subject matter to be shared. My host told me: "Do not worry. The Holy Spirit will give you the message." He was so right, but when the message came, I was shocked at its content.

The message was a strong call for unity and against proselytizing among the religious groups. I thought inwardly: "If I give this message, I'll never again be invited to Norway." As the group entered into praise and worship, the Holy Spirit quickened the message to my mind which

I was to share before proceeding with the main presentation:

> I have set a flame in Bergen. I will fan it into a mighty fire, but I must have trustworthy hands in which to place My fan. Therefore, I am waiting for my people to unite in My Spirit and to put all divisions from their midst. Then My fan will ignite a great fire in Bergen to My glory. Come My people and follow Me.

I gave that word and then shared the message the Lord had placed in my heart and mind the day before. At the close of the message I asked those who had been touched by the Holy Spirit to come forward. There was a mass movement to the platform. Many were healed; prayers of repentance came forth; some received the baptism with the Holy Spirit. What a joyous meeting!

The man responsible for bringing me to Bergen threw his arms around me saying: "Truly God sent you here this day. We have waited now for three years for someone to come forth with that message and we are so delighted. Praise His Name!"

We left the meeting to return to the host's home. I stood alone outside the garage as he drove the automobile into the building. Suddenly a voice spoke: "I am calling you to Norway. I will bring you back again soon. I will use you in that great thing I will do. Since you have humbled yourself under My hand in Denmark, I'm ready to use you."

Never before had such a thing happened to me. I was overwhelmed by the anointing that flooded through my whole being. Just then my host appeared. "Look at the sky," he said. The northern lights were dancing across the sky above the city. Suddenly a perfect circle was formed. How it could be I cannot explain, but there it stood like a mighty, gigantic halo over the whole city. My host looked heavenward and proclaimed: "What a confirmation that God has spoken to Bergen this night. Praise His Holy Name!"

I knew my life and ministry would never be the same as before. The Lord had truly touched me in a marvelous way. When I returned to the congregation in Idaho, they also knew their pastor had changed while in Scandinavia. As has already been said, there were two more visits to that area. The Lord used those visits to heal and deliver many from the bondages the enemy had placed upon the people. Between these visits, the Lord continued to open the ministry of healing and deliverance to me.

As I recounted earlier the result of my removal from the pulpit of the previous congregation was the formation of a new charismatic Lutheran congregation. Upon my return from Denmark and Norway, Satan made an outright challenge for control of the new congregation, thrusting me into ministry I felt ill-prepared to handle.

One evening, at approximately 10:30, the phone rang. The mother of a young man in the congregation requested that I come to her home immediately. There was fear in her voice and an urgency which could not be ignored. When queried as to why I should come, she replied, "Satan has my son. He is not himself. His eyes are very strange. He is cursing God and yelling at us. Something or someone has control over him." Further questioning ruled out the possibility of drugs or alcohol as the cause. I told her I would be right over.

As I drove the three miles to her home, I sought the Lord in prayer asking for guidance. My only preparation for what I was to meet was a recent reading of Don Basham's book DELIVER US FROM EVIL. I prayed: "Lord, what are You doing now? So much has happened so rapidly, I'm having trouble keeping up. What shall I do? I know nothing about the Satanic realm."

An answer came immediately: "Command the demons to identify themselves and command them out in My name." That was the total of my training to go against the forces of hell.

At the home, I found a situation which appeared to be rather normal. There was a calm atmosphere and the boy seemed in control of himself. I did sense some tension on the part of the young man but nothing unusual. I accepted a cup of coffee and shared in talk of the weather and such like. Nothing seemed to materialize (much to my relief) so I suggested I return home.

Upon reaching the door, I found my way blocked by the mother who pleaded with me not to leave. She said: "When your car entered the driveway, he suddenly calmed down. I know that the moment you leave, he will start again. Please do not leave."

I recalled what the Lord had said in response to my prayer, so I sat down, facing the boy. I asked him what had happened. He was totally unaware that anything had happened. I told him it was necessary to get to the cause and asked if he was willing to cooperate with me. His answer was affirmative, so I prayed a brief prayer asking the Lord for leading. At that time, I had no understanding of the need for preparation and the seeking of Divine protection to go against the forces of evil. Praise God

He protects us in our ignorance.

I looked the young man directly in the eyes and commanded any demonic force in him to manifest itself. Suddenly, the young man's eyes filled with something that I'd never seen in any person's eyes. His face distorted into a horrible mask of pure hatred and he slumped to the floor, his hands, arms and legs twisted and contorted into terrible shapes. Just as suddenly, he slipped into a catatonic condition, still twisted and contorted. Not a sound came from his lips.

I commanded the evil force to identify itself but nothing responded. After several futile efforts, I sat back to see what would happen. After a long period of time, the young man suddenly returned to normal, asking what had happened. Close questioning revealed that he knew little, if anything, about the whole episode.

I realized that I was confronted with a situation for which I needed answers beyond my training. I called a pastor whom I had been told was very cognizant of things concerning spiritual renewal. He said that he and his wife would come over immediately. I breathed a sigh of relief for now someone with an understanding of the whole state of affairs was on his way. To my dismay, I learned upon their arrival that they knew no more about deliverance than I. However, If I was willing to assume responsibility, they would assist in any way they could.

Once again I commanded the demonic force in the name and blood of the Lord Jesus Christ to make its presence known. As before, the young man slipped to the floor in a contorted catatonic state. After a number of commands directing the demonic force to identify itself, a taunting voice filled with hatred came from the young man saying: "My name is MURDER and I will kill everyone of you." I commanded the demon to come out in the name and blood of the Lord Jesus Christ. The demon replied: "I will not come out because he wants me and needs me." After a lengthy period of commanding, remitting the boy's sins and any other approach we could think of, the demon finally came out with a wrenching of the boy's body.

The young man sat up, utterly exhausted by the ordeal. While questioning him concerning his awareness during the episode, another demon arose, taking control of him with the same manifestations. Once again, I commanded in the name and blood of the Lord Jesus Christ. The demon identified itself as HATRED. This demon also left with a violent wrenching of the boy's body.

At approximately 4:00 A.M., the manifestation of demons came to a close. Fifteen to twenty different evil identities had been cast out. Each had cursed God, the boy's family and those of us who were working with him. We had truly faced the hatred of hell as the demonic forces controlled the boy's faculties and body members.

During the next three weeks, I was called out to three other homes to face similar situations. In each case, it was necessary to restrain the person with force as they possessed supernatural strength. Often the combined strength of four or five men was needed to restrain the possessed persons. Demons of drugs, alcohol, adultery, hatred, anger and a whole sordid list of others were cast out in the name and blood of the Lord Jesus Christ.

The events of that three week period proved to be but early skirmishes in the battle Satan was beginning to wage. A young man in the congregation began to show classic symptoms of schizophrenia. He would suddenly turn from being a doting husband and father into a morose, often ranting, abusive person. His wife and mother-in-law came seeking counsel as to what they should do. There seemed to be no apparent key to reveal the triggers bringing about the change. He himself came, realizing he needed help but reluctant to share much of his problem.

The situation steadily grew worse and became unbearable for the man. He confided that he was under demonic oppression over which he sometimes lost control. A time was set when I and several other men would meet with him to see if he could be set free. Little did I realize how great and strong the bondage was which held him. Had I known I might never have been involved in all that followed.

On the arranged evening, three other men and I went to the young man's home. He had not yet returned from his place of work though it was well past the usual time for his arrival at home. We waited for about forty-five minutes and then departed. Another hour and a half later a call was placed to the home and we learned he was just driving into the yard.

We rushed to the home, arriving just as he was preparing to leave again. I walked up to the automobile, looked in at the young man and saw a face contorted with rage and hatred. It was unbelievable that this was the same young man of such gentle nature who worshipped the Lord with us. He warned me to stay away from him, for, given any opportunity, he would kill me. I knew then he was fighting for control of his own self, warning me to be aware that he might lose control. He said the others were safe but before this night was over I would be dead.

After a few minutes he gained control of himself and agreed to go to the community hall where we met for worship services. In the car, he again warned me not to take my eyes from him for he was fighting an inner compulsion to kill me and he did not know how long he could keep the inner drive down. As a precaution he emptied his pockets of his knife or any other thing which might be used as a weapon. Gradually, the inner forces began to gain control and he pleaded that we stop the car so I could get out before the evil forces compelled him to attack. We assured him we would take every precaution, but felt we must stay with him so that he could be set free.

We arrived at the community hall but he refused to enter, demanding, instead, to go into an abandoned schoolhouse which stood alongside the community hall. We tried to explain we could not do that since it had been broken into a number of times and young people had been using it for drug sessions and other suspect purposes. We knew the police were keeping a close watch on that building. Furthermore, the building was locked and entry would be impossible without force.

He strode to the door of the building intent upon tearing it from its hinges. The evil forces within him were in full control and it was evident he would soon wrench the door loose. In desperation, I cried out: "In the name of Jesus Christ, I command you away from that door." He lurched back three steps, whirled about and came directly toward me. The other three men stepped forward to intercept him. He turned aside and rushed into the darkness of some trees. (It was a brilliant moonlit night and he was unable to remain in the light, seeking instead the shadow of the trees.)

He tore his shirt off, threw his shoes away and dropped on all fours. Growling like a wild animal and tearing huge clumps of grass and dirt from the ground, he would come to the line where the moonlight and darkness met and then retreat back into the darkness still growling and grunting as an enraged animal might. We called to him. He finally answered saying he wanted his brother to come and then he would meet with us.

His brother arrived shortly after our call. A look of disbelief came upon his face as he beheld his brother, who was still on hands and knees, tearing grass from the ground, grunting and howling like a wild animal. He called several times to him with no response. Suddenly the young man asked if that was his brother calling. When the answer was in the affirmative, he cried out: "Now is the time, you son-of-a-bitch, that you die!" He came hurtling out of the darkness straight toward me. He covered the last ten or twelve feet without even touching the ground.

In desperation I made the sign of the cross before him, which accomplished nothing. I turned my back to him to blunt the blow. He struck me with a force which knocked my glasses off and took me to my knees. He was clutching at my throat but was unable to close his fingers. Thank God, He made it impossible for those fingers to close, for my throat would have been ripped open with the strength he possessed.

His brother, a huge man, grasped the young man by the hair and began raining karate chops to his head and neck. I screamed: "Stop hitting him! Get him on the ground!" We finally wrestled him to the ground and pinned his arms and legs. Then began the long battle with the demonic forces holding control over the young man.

I commanded in the name and blood of the Lord Jesus Christ that the demon in control at that moment identify itself. The evil spirit, using the young man's voice, said: "My name is REDRUM."

"I do not know you. What is your name?" I demanded.

In great hatred and anger, the voice said: "DERTAH."

Again I responded that I did not know that name and commanded its real name. The voice rang out: "REGNA," and began to laugh tauntingly. I continued to command, in the name of Jesus Christ, that the demonic force identify itself in a language we could understand. Finally, the voice spat out: "You're so damn dumb you do not even know that I am talking bassackward. My name is MURDER and HATRED and ANGER and so many more you can never free him from us all."

With an outburst of expletives much too raw to repeat here, we were thrown about with such force it required all the strength the five of us could muster to control the young man. He weighed approximately one hundred sixty-five pounds. Such is the strength which comes when demonic forces are allowed to manifest themselves.

After a lengthy session, one demonic spirit left with a great sigh and wrenching of the young man's body. The men were ready to release him but I cautioned them not to do so for I knew the battle had barely begun. One man did release one of his arms and a fist grazed my jaw.

Once again, we were locked into battle with the forces of hell.

This time we were confronted by the demon of adultery which mocked us and taunted us saying: "I've made every one of your wives and you are too stupid to know it." This shows the cunning deviousness of Satan's evil workers. Apparently the demon hoped we would exert physical abuse on the young man in the mistaken thought he had really done what the demon said. (One must never accept what a demon says without first determining the validity of what has been said.) After several hours of intense struggle, many more manifestations appeared and were dealt with. The young man we had known from before was now in control of his own faculties.

Meeting later with the young man I learned how the Satanic forces had deceived him and taken control of his life. Much had come from his youth and early childhood days but the final control had taken place over a few months previous to the confrontation. He told how the demonic forces would appear to him in his sleep in order to prepare him for battle for the leadership of the congregation. These forces told him he would be used to determine who would be the spiritual authority in the congregation. Either Satan would have control or I had to die. With every defeat of Satan in the preceding confrontations, the need for killing me became more evident.

While he slept, the evil forces advised him of my every weakness and how it could be exploited to destroy me. At one point the demon had said to him: "The dumb fool thinks that making the sign of the cross will stop us. When he does that, go for his throat and we will kill him." The demonic forces tried to carry this out but God intervened and the young man was unable to close his fingers to choke me.

We face a cunning and powerful enemy. Though defeated, that enemy is never to be underestimated. Satan's work is not restricted to the world outside of the church. His strongest attacks are against the church - the apple of God's eye. He already holds the world in darkness and controls those outside of the church by that darkness. It is against the true church and the individual believer that the attentions of Satan and his evil workers are directed. They are well aware that it's time for war. What a tragedy such a large segment of Christianity is unaware of that reality.

Satan never relents in his attack upon a church which begins to threaten his kingdom. Apparently we were bothering him for he assailed us from all directions. Building programs were thwarted in devious ways. Internal problems continued to arise when least expected and from sources one would never have anticipated. Whenever the membership would increase, tension would also increase. Always there was an air of impending chaos as leadership rose among the laity and vied for control. Surely we were under the enemy's attack or we ourselves were out of God's favor.

A decision was reached in the Saturday evening men's prayer group to boldly approach the throne of God in prayer and ask for direct answers. The prayer group had been a powerful tool in the congregation. When we sought the Lord in prayer, blessings came. Likewise, when it weakened in its functions, there was a corresponding weakness in the congregation. The congregation seemed to be as healthy as its prayer groups.

The men gathered together in prayer, literally demanding answers as to why every plan and endeavor ended in chaos and often in the loss of members. We announced to the Lord that we would remain in prayer until we had answers. There was little need for that announcement for the Lord answered quite rapidly.

One of the men spoke these words: "Some in your midst have sought to build to man's glory and not to mine. My glory I will not give to any man." We were stunned. We believed that all of the members desired to build to the glory of God. We humbly came before the Lord in repentance, asking forgiveness and His guidance. Again, prayers were offered and the question was set before Him: "Should we disband the congregation?" His reply was gentle but firm: "Follow Me and I will lead you to that place which I have chosen for you." A short while later the congregation purchased an existing church facility. The deliverance ministry was continued by an elder of the church and me in the new church office. A large number of those ministered to were not members of the congregation. We were still using an "exhaling" method and while there was little, if any, violence, there was, also, very little being accomplished. Then came a dramatic change.

One evening, during the service, a member of the congregation shared how she seemed to be preoccupied and disassociated from the worship. At the close of the meeting, she raised her hand for prayer, saying: "Something very strange is going on. I have been here all evening yet I have been unable to participate. I have been with you yet not a part of you. Please pray for me."

I asked her to come forward and placed a chair for her to be seated. My intention was to ask the whole group to come and lift her in intercession to the Lord. As she sat down, the Holy Spirit spoke to me: "Command the demonic spirit in her to come out in the name and the blood of the Lord Jesus Christ."

I thought: "Oh no, Lord, not that. Not here in a public service." But I followed the Spirit's bidding and commanded any evil spirit possessing her to come out in the name and blood of the Lord Jesus Christ. Immediately, something took control. Her face contorted into a mask of intense hatred and she lunged from the chair towards me, her arms outstretched, her hands clutching towards my throat, mutterings of hatred and murder rolled from her lips. The forces of hell had been loosed in her.

Two men standing by the chair restrained her and in the wrestling match which ensued all fell to the floor. She was held down by several persons and then a violent procession of demons of hatred, murder, rejection, anger and many others began. After a long period of time, all became quiet and peace came to her soul and mind. Raising her arms, she praised God, thanking Him that she was free - free of the depression which had tormented her most of her life.

Now the deliverance ministry was public. Word spread rapidly of what had occurred. The gossips had their day, but, praise God, the word also went out to others who knew they needed help and they began to come.

This same woman returned to a later meeting for more ministry, realizing she was not totally free. Another violent deliverance took place and, again, after a period of time, the manifestations ceased. At this same meeting, suddenly and without warning, another young woman in the congregation arose crying out: "Help me!" I looked at her and saw a vacant look in her eyes. A complete change took place in her countenance as something took control of her. She slumped to the floor muttering words of hatred and anger. Once again, the violent procession of demonic forces; once again, the superhuman strength needing restraint; once again, a number of violent demons cast out before she became quiet.

By now people were coming to the evening services seeking freedom from various bondages. All were of a violent nature since we had not yet learned how to prevent the violent manifestations so the curious also came to see the latest show. The public display of deliverance was too much for some of the members and they left to find quiet and dignified churches. Satan seized the opportunity to warm up the gossip mills and soon all kinds of wild rumors were flowing concerning the congregation.

Some in the community said our church was Satan's church and that we worshipped him. People were warned to stay away for surely they would become demon possessed if they were to attend the services. Others said we were so busy chasing demons we did not have time to praise or worship the Lord Jesus Christ.

Much to the contrary, I was seeking for a balance where all aspects of ministry would be carried out. But it's most difficult to combat the forces of evil when the gossip mills spew out their vile rumors and half-truths. The most damaging accusations came from some who never attended the services and had never attended a deliverance session or never consulted with those involved in the ministry. I am sure that these men were sincere in their efforts and were convinced it was pleasing in the sight of God.

After the experience with the young man, I wondered about the physical demands of the deliverance ministry. I was not a young man and I could not see myself continuing to wrestle a couple of nights a week with men much younger than myself. Also, I began to question my role in such a ministry. I could not see how I could minister to the needs of a congregation and continue to be involved in violent deliverances. Once again, I sought the Lord for answers. I was hoping the answer would be a release from all forms of deliverance ministry. No release came but the number of cases began to drop.

I had come into contact with another minister who was casting out demonic forces through a non-violent method. A young woman came to me suffering with serious epileptic seizures. I asked her if she would meet with this man in order to be set free and to allow me an opportunity to observe this method. Both of them agreed.

The method was rather simple, involving the inhaling of air and then exhaling it as the demonic forces are commanded out. The guidance of the Holy Spirit was depended upon to discern what demonic forces should be commanded out.

At the close of the session, we were told she would be free of the tormenting demonic forces. I must admit I was not convinced on the basis of what I had seen but was willing to allow time to be the determining factor. I also observed that the young woman herself had not been convinced of the validity of the method and therefore did not fully cooperate. Since that time, she's experienced further violent seizures. She also joined another congregation and I have not had the opportunity to minister to her again.

Much valuable information was gained from my contacts with this man concerning the general areas of demonic functioning. I learned how one seeks and recognizes the gift of discerning. I am thankful for the valuable insights gained through this fellow minister.

Taking these new insights, I sought to adapt them to my counseling as people continued to come for help. In many cases, remarkable things happened and many were set free. In other cases, it seemed nothing changed and people left disappointed. In one or two cases, it almost seemed things worsened. I have now come to the realization I was undoubtedly working with a psychological approach and most likely was being deceived by the spirit of psychology. Since that time, I have seen many spirits of psychology forced to leave Christians when commanded in the authority of the name of Jesus Christ and the power of His shed blood.

I sought the Lord for deeper insights into the control of violence. I was convinced there must be some way to prevent it without the uncertainties of psychological applications. Surely our Lord would open a way if we sought diligently. I purchased every book available that might shed some light on the matter. I listened to other men's tapes always adding to my storehouse of knowledge.

During my search I met a man who had traveled widely in his search for information on deliverance. Having retired from the business world, he had become involved in a nursing home ministry. In this outreach, he encountered powerful forces which hindered his witnessing to many in those homes who were under heavy bondage. He set out in search of information. This eventually led him to Chicago where he observed the ministry of Pastor Wynn Worley. While there he purchased a book by Pastor Worley.

After purchasing the book, he was convinced the Holy Spirit instructed him to give four of the books to selected pastors in his home area in Idaho. One of the names given him was mine. When he arrived with the book and explained the situation, I asked him: "Are you aware that I have been active in this kind of ministry for a considerable period of time?" (We had known one another for a long period but had never reached the point of ministering together.)

He responded he had heard but had not felt moved to investigate. He was invited to attend and soon became actively involved in the ministry. Through his financial support and involvement, we were able to gather information from others involved in healing and deliverance ministries. That information has proved invaluable as time has gone on.

The approach to inner-healing and deliverance began to move into a team method involving the retired businessman, Shirley and me. The Holy Spirit drew my attention to the work of God's angels as recorded in the scriptures. I was particularly drawn to Hebrews 1:13,14: "But to which of the angels said he at anytime, Sit on my right hand, until I make thine enemies thy footstool? Are they not all ministering spirits, sent forth to minister for them who shall be heirs of salvation?" The Greek text seems to imply that angels are ministering spirits sent to "give service" to those who shall be heirs of salvation. After much prayer by all concerned, the decision was reached to ask the heavenly Father to assign angels who would restrain the body and members of those receiving ministry.

At the first session where this request was made, we were amazed at the result. The amazement arose from the fact that the counselee was a person with whom we had counseled before. He had experienced violent manifestations in the previous sessions. In this session, manifestations of anger arose but the person was unable to rise from his chair. We could almost picture chains binding him down. After the session, he confided that his arms felt as though five thousand pound weights were attached and some kind of binding secured his arms, legs and chest.

The Lord had led us into non-violent deliverance. No longer were we faced with the threat of violence in the sessions. No longer did the people leave the sessions with bruises on arms and legs from the hands of people restraining the violent forces being manifested. This is not to say that those counseled did not experience a ravaging by unclean spirits. However, the manifestation was very subdued. The only problem was to determine when the unclean spirits were gone since we had come to depend on the manifestations. The solution was the gift of discerning which began to operate more fully.

The requests for ministry increased each week. Members of the congregation began to feel uneasy with the deliverance ministry being conducted in the public worship services. To quiet this, people desiring ministry in the area of inner-healing and deliverance were urged to arrange for counseling on weekdays. Soon the days were filled. Several teams of counselors were raised up to work with people in the public services and to steer them into the weekday schedule.

At this point a vital lesson was learned. It became apparent that something was amiss. Some came once and were not seen again. Some came on several occasions but did not seem to improve though visible manifestations of departing unclean spirits were observed. After much prayer, we were impressed that the problem was centered on the relationship of those receiving ministry with the Lord Jesus Christ. We began to question each counselee closely concerning their submission to the lordship of Jesus Christ. We were surprised when many were unable to make a strong commitment.

Soon the number of counselees began to drop. It was most apparent the Holy Spirit was leading us to see the enemy was flooding us with people to consume our time and to draw us away from the work of the Lord's kingdom. Two factors were set before us: First, only Christians are capable of remaining free; secondly, the enemy will steer people to ministers of deliverance who, once ministered to, cannot remain free. This is done in order to consume time needed in kingdom work.

The fruit of the ministry began to appear more abundantly. The counseling appointments began to reflect all levels of Christian maturity. They ranged from relatively new Christians to mature workers of the Lord including ministers and their wives.

As is true in all ministries, not all who came were delivered and healed. Only the Lord knows the answer as to why. I am sure our lack of knowledge and ineptness were contributing factors in these seeming failures. Likewise, our zeal may have moved us ahead of the Lord's timetable for some of those receiving ministry. But as our knowledge increased and as the gifting of the Holy Spirit was recognized and employed, the failure rate dropped significantly. It would be beautiful to be able to say every person ministered to received total healing and freedom. But that is not always the case because of the variables involving the Lord, the counselor and the counselee.

The inner-healing/deliverance ministry requires a great expenditure of time on the part of those providing such counseling. The demands of the counseling load and the needs of the parish came into conflict. Time was needed to train men and women to help carry the counseling load. Many came forward to be used in the deliverance outreach. Once involved, most sought a gracious way out. Truly, the Lord must call one to this kind of ministry. Likewise, He alone equips those whom He calls. That is not to say experienced counselors do not have insights to share; however, the effective counselor in inner-healing/ deliverance is called and gifted by God, the Holy Spirit. We ultimately saw three teams of two persons each ministering in the area of deliverance. These teams ministered both privately and in the public services.

Again, it is unbelievable how the Satanic realm is able to distort the honest and sincere efforts of dedicated workers of the Lord. There was a persistent rumor within the community that the congregation was involved in witchcraft and Satan worship. We were even accused of holding black mass because counseling continued into the late hours on worship nights. People who expressed interest in the congregation were advised by others that membership demanded a deliverance session by the pastor. The tragedy is not so much in there being accusations as in the fact Christians believed the lies without determining their validity. However, in spite of the adverse publicity, word of mouth brought a continuous flow of people seeking counseling and ministry.

One aspect of my ministry continued to perplex me. Throughout my ministry I desired to see healings take place in the public worship services. I truly believed that healing was one of the signs which should follow those who believe. I had seen the confirmation of signs following in the deliverances, but why was there a lack of consistent healings?

At one point in my ministry I felt the Lord had acknowledged my prayers for a healing ministry. Through a stupid action on my part my left leg was severely damaged between the bumpers of two automobiles. Fortunately, when the bumpers met they were at an angle which saved the bone from being crushed. The doctor's prognosis was three or four weeks on crutches.

About one week after the accident, I was lying on the bed in a great deal of pain, waiting for the pain-killer to take effect. I prayed: "Lord, if You have a special ministry for me, I would like a healing ministry," Suddenly, a powerful anointing moved through my body. Its manifestation baffled me for only one-half of my body was affected. The power flowed through the left side only and seemed to settle in the injured leg. The pain stopped immediately and no more pain pills were taken. Within a few days the crutches were discarded. I now knew the Lord still desires to heal, not only through medical resources, but also through direct divine intervention. However, my praying for the sick bore little fruit.

Following dismissal from pulpit duties in the first congregation and the formation of the new one, I stepped out in faith to pray for healings during the public services. However, my thinking at the time was somewhat clouded. I believed healing and deliverance constituted

42

two separate ministries. I had even prayed asking for a healing ministry but not one of deliverance. I began to see limited results but there was no consistency. Doubt seemed to permeate each effort: "Would the person be healed? Did he/she have enough faith? Do I have enough faith?" The deliverance ministry was producing abundant fruit. People were being set free as bondages were lifted, but the healing ministry sputtered along.

During a prayer session involving several men, we asked the Lord why the healing ministry was so inconsistent. Similar cases would see one healed while another seemed untouched. In the midst of the prayer, these words were impressed upon my mind: "My son, why do you continually call upon Me to come down and touch and heal? I have completed My work upon the cross. I have commissioned and empowered all believers to go forth and heal. Why is it that you do not command illnesses and infirmities with the same authority and power that you command demons to leave?"

I was stunned. At that moment, I came to realize healing and deliverance were one and the same ministries. Now I was able to see one reason why some do not see the manifestations of healing. The root of the problem was not being dealt with. Much of what was seen as healing ministry was little more than a band-aid, medicine which provided surface healing but did not touch the festering sore beneath.

Now the words of our Lord in Matthew 21:21,22 took on new meanings: "... if ye shall say unto this mountain, Be thou removed, and be thou cast into the sea; it shall be done. And all things, whatsoever ye shall ask in prayer, believing, ye shall receive." It was time to begin addressing the mountains in people's lives. From that moment, the healing aspect of our ministry became much more fruitful. Manifestations of healing were much more consistent.

Beginning in 1975, various prophetic messages came to the charismatic Lutheran church I was pastoring. It was not unusual, therefore, for someone to give a prophetic message but this one, given in the closing days of May, 1979, was life-changing in its import:

> My people are perishing for lack of knowledge. My people have been perishing for years for lack of knowledge. Now, My son, go forth — go forth into all the nations, all the lands hereabout and preach My word. Preach it in its purity. I have told you before to hold back nothing. Go out and tell everyone that you meet, how

the enemy has stolen My people. Save My children, for they are perishing daily. They are being taken away from Me by the enemy. Save them now. Hold back not one thing. Do not fear man. Go in My strength. My son, go with the message that I have given you. I have prepared you. My son, go! Go this night and save My little ones. Feed My sheep."

Many times my wife, Shirley, and I had received words of comfort and exhortation concerning the ministry for that congregation and community. But the strength of this message was that we were to go. I was very close to these people. We had shared pain and suffering; joy and victory; and the continuing presence of the Lord. This process had "weeded-out" the uncommitted. I had begun to feel change was coming but now I knew some step of obedience would soon be required.

I believe that message affirms the reality of spiritual warfare which is being waged against the body of Christ. It further affirms the call of God to His Church to become actively involved in that warfare. It is definitely time for war. It is time for the church to awaken to the reality that there is a current warfare which exists between Satan and the body of Christ.

****

Part II: (BIBLICAL & HISTORICAL)

CHAPTER 2

SPIRITUAL WARFARE

I have no doubt that a state of war exists between the kingdom of God and the principalities of Satan. I have come to this conviction through experience and the study of Scripture. Since it is possible, even likely, that many who read this will not be of that same mind, I feel it important to trace this spiritual warfare from its beginnings to the present.

I consider the issue of salvation on a broader basis than moving souls from the kingdom of darkness to the kingdom of light. I also see the whole area of sanctification (i.e. the Christian walk) as more than a matter of obedience on the part of the Christian. My experiences as a parish minister and a Christian counselor persuade me that a state of spiritual warfare does presently exist, that it is waged against every Christian (regardless of a Christian's awareness of its reality) and that every facet of the Christian's life is subject to that warfare. To ignore this reality is to open the Christian and the whole body of Christ to the ravages of Satan - God's enemy and the enemy of God's people.

This great spiritual conflict, which seldom excludes physical warfare, began in the heavenly realm with Lucifer who sought to become the equal of God in all ways.

> How art thou fallen from heaven, O Lucifer, son of the morning! How art thou cut down to the ground, which didst weaken the nations! For thou hast said in thine heart, I will ascend into heaven, I will exalt my throne above the stars of God: I will sit also upon the mount of the congregation, in the sides of the north: I will ascend above the heights of the clouds: I will be like the Most High. [Isaiah 14:12-14]

How Lucifer could reason in this manner is difficult to comprehend, especially considering the perfection in which he dwelt. Yet, we see evidence of this same false reasoning by those among us who claim an earthly perfection like that known by Lucifer in the heavenly realms. When men claim to be unable to sin, to possess perfect faith or to be in a select company of perfected believers, they are walking in a path dangerously similar to Lucifer's line of reasoning. Self-exaltation is a very strong temptation to overcome.

Lucifer's rebellion led to the fall of a third of the angelic hosts and pitted this army against Michael (another archangel) and the angels who continued to serve God

> ...there was war in heaven: Michael and his angels fought against the dragon: and the dragon fought and his angels, and prevailed not: neither was their place found anymore in heaven and the great dragon was cast out, that old serpent, called the devil, and Satan which deceiveth the whole world; he was cast out into the earth, and his angels were cast out with him. [Rev. 12:7-9]

This great battle in heaven culminated in defeat for Satan and his host. However, the state of war did not cease; it simply moved from heaven to earth.

The defeat of Satan in the heavenly realms and his banishment to earth loosed his fury upon all mankind. God's word records the history of this fact. Alfred Edersheim writes of this in his Bible History:

> The measure of the sin of the nations who occupied Palestine was now full (Gen. 15:13-16,) and the storm of judgment was to sweep them away. For this purpose Israel, to whom God in His mercy had given the land, was to be employed -- but only insofar as the people realized its calling to dedicate the land unto the Lord. On the ruins of what not only symbolized but at the time really was the kingdom of Satan, the theocracy was to be up built. Instead of that focus when the vilest heathenism overspread the world, the kingdom of God was to be established, with the opposite mission of sending the light of truth to the remotest parts of the earth. [Edersheim, p. 109,110]

I believe Edersheim captured the reality of the existing warfare between the kingdom of God and the kingdom of Satan. This warfare transcended physical conflict to encompass worship and the daily lives of the people. The very thoughts of the people were touched by the supernatural ramifications of the spiritual warfare which raged throughout the Old Testament record.

Satan's battle plan turned from outright, frontal attack upon the angelic host of God to devious attempts to thwart every plan of God concerning earth. God created Adam and Eve on earth with a specific directive:

> ... Be fruitful, and multiply, and replenish the earth, and subdue it; and have dominion over the fish of the sea, and over the fowl of the air, and over every living thing upon the earth. [Gen. 1:28]

Adam was given dominion over every living thing upon the earth. Satan immediately determined to destroy God's plan. With cunning deceit, he probed for Eve's weakest point: "Yea, hath God said, Ye shall not eat of every tree in the garden?" [Gen. 3:1] A seed of doubt was planted, even though Eve sought to speak God's words concerning the tree in the middle of the garden: "Ye shall not eat of it, neither shall ye touch it, lest ye die." [Gen. 3:3] Satan skillfully nurtured that seed:

> Ye shall not surely die: for God doth know that in the day ye eat thereof, then your eyes shall be opened, and ye shall be as gods, knowing good and evil. [Gen.3:4,5]

Satan had planted yet another seed - equality with God and self-exaltation. Both seeds took root and Eve "took of the fruit thereof and did eat, and gave also unto her husband with her, and he did eat." [Gen. 3:6] Adam, who had been given dominion over all living things upon the earth, never questioned Eve - never exercised his leadership responsibility. He ate and in that action gave over his dominion to Satan. It appeared, for all practical purposes, God's plan was thwarted.

Thus the sin principle was initiated in man. And it is to this sin principle that satan always appeals - tempting, deceiving, threatening, lying, drawing - in the effort to gain man's participation in the spiritual warfare he had initiated in the heavenlies. While it is true Satan's ultimate conflict is against God, the battle ground is the body, soul and spirit of man.

God responded to Satan's attack in Genesis 3. To the serpent He said:

> ...thou art cursed above all cattle, and above every beast of the field; ...and I will put enmity between thee and the

47

woman, and between thy seed and her seed; it shall bruise thy head, and thou shalt bruise his heel. [v. 14,15]

To the woman He said:

I will greatly multiply thy sorrow and thy conception; in sorrow thou shalt bring forth children; and thy desire shall be to thy husband, and he shall rule over thee. [v. 16]

To the man He said:

...cursed is the ground for thy sake; in sorrow shalt thou eat of it all the days of thy life ... in the sweat of thy face shalt thou eat bread, till thou return unto the ground; [v. 17-19]

The ongoing state of spiritual war can be seen in God's response, especially in the words spoken to Satan concerning his seed and Eve's seed. This statement transcends the enmity between man and serpent. It predicts the spiritual warfare to be waged by Satan against all of mankind and against God's eternal plan of salvation. That enmity and that plan exist to this very day.

After the fall, Satan's corruptive work among men continued to manifest itself until God proclaimed:

...The end of all flesh is come before Me; for the earth is filled with violence through them; and behold, I will destroy them with the earth. [Gen. 6:13]

It would seem Satan was close to victory since for God to destroy His own creation would seem to be an utter defeat for God. But Satan failed to comprehend the infinite wisdom of God.

After the great flood and the ark had settled upon solid ground, Noah stepped out to build an alter to God on a newly cleansed earth. Looking upon Noah's sacrifice of worship:

...the Lord said in His heart, I will not again curse the ground any more for man's sake, for that the imagination of man's hearts is evil from his youth; neither will I again smite any more every thing living as I have done. [Gen.8:21]

48

The fallen leader and his evil angelic army did not perish in the flood, and God knew full well that man would continue to fall victim to Satan's wiles. This is borne out in the spiritual warfare which continued after Noah led his family from the ark. Noah became drunk on his own wine and in his drunkenness lay in his tent naked and exposed. His son Ham mocked his father by telling his brothers. A sober Noah cursed Canaan, the son of Ham: "... cursed be Canaan; a servant of servants shall he be unto his brethren." [Gen. 9:25] Once again, the forces of evil had struck against God's plan for mankind.

There seems to be a period of time when, for all practical purposes, most men knew God and His desires for their lives. However, once again, Satan's influence was manifested in the person of Nimrod, the grandson of Ham. Scripture says that Nimrod "was a mighty hunter before the Lord; ...and the beginning of his kingdom was Babel, and Erech, and Accad, and Calneh, in the land of Shinar." [Gen. 10:9,10] On page 3 of his booklet The Mystery of Iniquity, Mr. Griffin states: "Strong's Concordance shows that the Hebrew word 'pariym,' translated 'before' in this passage, should be translated 'against.' Yes, Nimrod was clearly against God." Griffin quotes the historian Alexander Hyslop as writing:

> The amazing extent of the worship of this man (Nimrod) indicates something very extra-ordinary in his charac-ter; and there is ample reason to believe, that in his own day he was an object of high popularity. Though by setting up as king, Nimrod invaded the patriarchal sys-tem, ... (page 1.) According to the system Nimrod was the grand instrument in introducing, men were led to believe that a real spiritual change of heart was unnec-essary, and that as far as change was needful, they could be regenerated by mere external means ... (He) led mankind to seek their chief good in sensual enjoyment, and showed them how they might enjoy the pleasure of sin without any fear of the wrath of a holy God. (page 3.)

According to Griffin, the people of Nimrod's day who rejected God fell into false beliefs, and "these were the beliefs promulgated by Nimrod and which gave him even more power over the people. He became the priest of the sun god or Bol-kahn, which means the priest of Baal. He was therefore the priest of devil worship." (page 4.) It was under Nimrod's guidance that the people were moved to say:

> ... let us build us a city and a tower, whose top may reach unto heaven; and let us make us a name, lest we be

scattered abroad upon the face of the whole earth. [Gen 11:4]

Because of Satan's influence upon men, God was forced to intercede. He destroyed the tower, confounded their language and scattered them upon the face of the earth. God's action hindered Satan's warfare, but it did not stop it. Semiiramis, the wife of Nimrod,

> ... is known to have impressed upon them (the people) the image of her own depraved and polluted mind. That beautiful but abandoned queen of Babylon was not only herself a paragon of unbridled lust and licentiousness, but in the mysteries which she had a chief hand in forming, she was worshipped as Rhea, the great mother of the gods, with such atrocious rites as identified her with Venus, the mother of all impurity ... (quoted from Hyslop by Griffin, page 5.)

The next step in God's plan was a man named Abraham through whom He would establish a nation. To Abraham He said:

> Get thee out of thy country, and from thy kindred, and from thy father's house, unto a land that I will show thee, and I will bless thee, and make thy name great; and thou shalt be a blessing. [Gen. 12:1-2]

The contrast in the characters of Nimrod and Abraham is important to note: Nimrod made a city to reach heaven - Abraham sought a city made by God; Nimrod gathered all to himself in disobedience to God - Abraham left all in obedience to God; Nimrod trusted in his own abilities - Abraham trusted only in God. This affords us insight as to how some men become the tools of Satan and others become the vessels of God.

However, the righteousness of Abraham's character did not prevent Satan influencing the mind of Abraham. Fearing for his life, Abraham proposed Sarah tell a lie:

> And it came to pass, when he was come near to enter into Egypt, that he said unto Sarah his wife, Behold now, I know that thou art a fair woman to look upon: Therefore it shall come to pass, when the Egyptians shall see thee, that they shall say, This is his wife: and they will kill me, but they will save thee alive. Say, I pray thee, thou art my sister: that it may be well with me for thy sake; and my

soul shall live because of thee. [Gen. 12:11-13]

Jesus declared to his disciples that Satan is the father of lies. Satan used the twin weapons of fear and falsehood to weaken God's man and, hopefully, thwart the establishment of a people true to God. God intervened by sending plagues upon Pharaoh who then commanded Abraham to take Sarah and leave.

Satan is persistent in his warfare. A battle lost merely calls for another. He turned next to strife and division in an effort to stop God's plan. The wealth of Lot and Abraham had become so great,

> ...the land was not able to bear them, that they might dwell together ... and there was strife between the herdsmen of Abraham's cattle and the herdsmen of Lot's cattle. [Gen.13:6,7]

This time Abraham's godly character prevailed. Satan employed a divide-and-conquer tactic, but Abraham countered it by dividing the land between Lot and himself and having them go separate ways. Satan's battle plan was turned aside but he persevered in the warfare.

Satan launched an attack of doubt upon God's plan by singling out Sarah. Since she had not conceived and given birth to children, she formulated a plan to expedite God's promise. Sarah convinced Abraham to produce a child through, Hagar her maid. (Considering the sexual inclinations of most men and Satan's pervasive influence, Sarah probably didn't have to work too hard to persuade Abraham.)

Out of this union came Ishmael of whom an angel of the Lord said:

> And he will be a wild man; his hand will be against every man, and every man's hand against him; and he shall dwell in the presence of all his brethren. [Gen. 16:12]

Though Abraham looked upon Ishmael as his heir, God's plan was not to be sidetracked by the doubt which brought about his birth. Both he and his mother were sent out from the family. However, God remembered Hagar and His promise that out of Ishmael would come a great nation. Much of the peninsula between the Euphrates, the Straits of Suez, and the Red Sea was populated by his descendants.

51

Just as God's plan unfolds in the lives of men and women faithfully following Him, so also Satan's spiritual warfare is waged against God and His people through men and women. An example of these parallel patterns of warfare is seen in the twins, Jacob and Esau. The life-long enmity between the brothers developed early because of parental favoritism. When Esau sold the birthright and Jacob stole the patriarchal blessing, the stage was set for fratricidal warfare. Esau would probably have murdered his brother if Jacob had not fled. The enmity continued through the ages, undoubtedly fueled by Satan's determination to void the purposes of God set in the Israelites. We find the Edomites (Esau's descendants) opposing the children of Israel (Jacob) on the way to the promised land; invading Israel during the reigns of Saul, David and Solomon; they joined with Nebuchadnezzar in razing Jerusalem with unbelievable slaughter. As prophesied to Rebekah, two nations came from her womb: one manifested continual hatred and warfare against God and His people; the other sought, imperfectly perhaps, the divine will.

Spiritual warfare reared its head again in the treatment Joseph received at the hands of his brothers. Surely, the diabolical desire to murder and lie cannot be solely attributed to carnal natures. Satan must have had his hand in but little did he realize that the sale of a teenage boy into slavery would boomerang and actually advance God's plan to produce a nation. Joseph was to find favor in the sight of the Pharaoh opening the way for Jacob and his family to come into Egypt and setting the stage for the unfolding of God's plan. [See Gen. 37-50]

The long term protection of Egypt permitted Israel to become numerous in people and herds. In time a pharaoh came to the throne who "knew not Joseph." Satan promoted fear in this man in order to launch another plan of attack." [Exodus 1:7] Fearful that the Israelites would join an enemy in war against Egypt, Pharaoh enslaved them and set them to building the treasury cities. Still the Israelites increased in number. Then a diabolical idea formed in Pharaoh's mind: decree that the midwives should destroy every male child born of the Israelites. But the midwives feared God, disobeyed the decree and saved the men children alive. Finally, in absolute frustration, Pharaoh "... charged all his people, saying, Every son that is born ye shall cast into the river, and every daughter ye shall save alive." [Exodus 1:22] How the innocent suffer in all warfare!

By now we are beginning to learn that even devil-inspired ideas cannot prevent the purposes of God. In fact, God turns those very ideas into a means of furthering His own plans. The sister of Pharaoh found a Hebrew child floating among the reeds of a river in a pitched basket. The child's sister was watching nearby. She offered to find a Hebrew woman to nurse the baby. That woman was, of course, the child's mother. So it was the child, Moses, was nurtured by a Jewish mother and matured in the courts of Pharaoh. In this child and the Pharaoh next to rise to power the spiritual warfare between God and Satan would be manifested in an intense conflict of wills.

Could it have been that though he was raised as Egyptian royalty, Moses sensed some destiny as the one to free God's people, the Israelites? In any case, he took matters into his own hands and committed murder. The handiwork of Satan is easily seen since he is a murderer from the beginning. Besides provoking another murder, the result would be the end of God's chosen man and the hinderance of God's purposes. Moses fled into Midian and it was there God called him and Moses responded.

In the confrontation between Moses and Pharaoh the evidence of spiritual warfare can be clearly seen. Moses and Aaron came before Pharaoh to ask permission for the Hebrews to go to the desert to worship. When Pharaoh refused, Moses, as directed by God, cast down Aaron's rod before Pharaoh and his priests. Striking the ground it became a serpent. Not to be outdone, the priests of Pharaoh used Satanic witchcraft and cast down rods which also became serpents. However, to their great dismay, they witnessed the greater power of God as Aaron's rod swallowed the serpents of the priests.

The warfare continued through plagues of frogs, lice, flies, death of cattle, boils, hail, locust, darkness, and finally the death of all the first-born Egyptians. Pharaoh commanded Moses to take the Israelites out of Egypt. However, the evil control over his mind drove him to seek a means of slaying God's people. Gathering his army he pursued God's people to the Red Sea in order to trap them against the sea to be slaughtered. The power of God was manifested in the sea parting to allow God's people to cross over but when Pharaoh's men entered the sea, it closed again and all were destroyed.

Just before calamity overcame them, the Egyptians apparently recognized the spiritual aspects of the warfare: "Let us flee from the face of Israel; for the Lord fights for them against the Egyptians." [Exodus 14:25] This is echoed by Moses and the Israelites when they gave the same witness:

> ... the Lord is a man of war, the Lord is his name.
> Pharaoh's chariots and his host hath he cast into the sea;

his chosen captains also are drowned in the Red Sea."
[Exodus 15:3,4]

Thus God brought His people out of bondage and thwarted Satan's plan to destroy His program for the nation. But the warfare did not cease.

Before they came to Mt. Sinai the Israelites fought their first pitched battle. The Amalekites, believed to be among the descendants of Esau, attacked at Rephidim. By the hand of the Lord, Joshua and his army prevailed and brought great destruction upon the Amalekites. But this was not the end of these implacable foes. They were to cause problems to future generations because their hatred was not only against the Israelites but actually against God. Moses seemed to understand this aspect of the warfare when he erected a memorial altar. He said:

"Because a hand was against the throne of the Lord, the Lord will be at war against the Amalekites from generation to generation." [Ex. 17:16, NIV alternate reading.]

As difficult as these battles were, they were minor when compared to the warfare within the people of God. Satan's influence turned the Israelites to the desires of their flesh rather than trusting God. They murmured against God and Moses because they lacked water - God provided them a miraculous supply of water. They murmured for lack of food - God provided manna. They complained because they were tired of eating manna - He sent them quail. Continually they gave in to the appetites and desires of the flesh, murmuring and turning against Moses and against God.

Even as God gave Moses the tablets of stone containing the law, the warfare continued at the base of the mountain. Because Moses did not return at the time the people believed he should, they gathered together and told Aaron to "make us gods which shall go before us, for as for this Moses, we do not know what has become of him." [Exodus 32:1] Aaron did as they requested, fashioning a golden calf from their gold, and the people danced and committed great sin before it. Satan must have rejoiced. The influence of the master of evil controlled the people as they danced and involved themselves in sexual promiscuity before the face of the living God.

It may be argued by some that there is no direct evidence this lapse into idolatry was the result of Satan's influence. Man can think up plenty of evil on his own, it is true, but New Testament revelation shows the clear link to Satan. Paul reveals that when sacrifices are made before idols, they are, in fact, being offered to devils (1 Cor 10:19-21.) Considering the examples of God's drastic efforts to purge the Israelites of every taint of idolatry, it is little wonder that Paul exhorted the Corinthians to "flee from idolatry."

Spiritual warfare is never to be taken lightly; casualties will result and are usually to be found in the world of flesh and bone.

> Then Moses stood in the gate of the camp, and said, who is on the Lord's side? Let him come unto me. And all the sons of Levi gathered themselves together unto him. And he said unto them, thus saith the Lord God of Israel, Put every man his sword by his side, and go in and out from gate to gate throughout the camp, and slay every man his brother, and every man his companion, and every man his neighbor .. and there fell of the people that day about three thousand men." [Exodus 32:26-28]

While still on the Mount, God's promises to Moses indicate His understanding of the potential danger from the demon worship in the conquered lands:

> Take heed to thyself, lest thou make a covenant with the inhabitants of the land whither thou goest, lest it be for a snare in the midst of thee: But ye shall destroy their altars, break their images, and cut down their groves. For thou shalt worship no other god, for the Lord, whose name is Jealous, is a jealous God." [Exodus 34:12-14]

God's words leave little doubt that a state of spiritual warfare would continue between a people who would do God's will, worshipping Him in truth, and a people who served the will of Satan and worshipped in pagan rites.

The promised land stands in Scripture as a crucial test for God's people and their will to participate in spiritual warfare. They camped at the southern part of the land and God commanded Moses to send out men to scout the land of Canaan. Moses responded by sending out leaders of the tribes of Israel. Upon returning to Moses and Aaron, they reported the land was truly one of milk and honey. That was the good news - then came the bad news: the people who lived there were powerful and lived in fortified cities. One man, Caleb, "stilled the people before Moses and said, Let us go up at once, and possess it; for we are well able to overcome it." (Num. 13:30) But the other scouts lied as to what they had seen reporting that in comparison to the inhabitants of the land, the Isarelites were as grasshoppers.

Fear gripped the whole nation of Israel. They wept and complained and talked of electing someone to take them back to Egypt. Caleb, now joined by Joshua, strongly exhorted the people to trust the Lord:

> The land which we passed through to search it, is an exceeding good land. If the Lord delight in us, then He will bring us into this land, and give it us ... Only rebel not ye against the Lord, neither fear ye the people of the land; for they are bread for us; their defense is departed from them, and the Lord is with us; fear them not. [Num.14:7-9]

The response of the people was to chose the lie (even as Adam and Eve in Eden's garden) and attempt to stone their leaders. The response of Moses and Aaron was to prostate themselves before the Tabernacle. But the response of God pinpointed this event as a spiritual battle. The Lord's glory appeared and He spoke:

> Because all those men which have seen my glory and my miracles, which I did in Egypt and in the wilderness, and have tempted me now these ten times, and have not harkened to my voice; surely they shall not see the land which I swore unto their fathers, neither shall any of them that provoked me see it. But my servant Caleb, because he had another spirit with him, and hath followed me fully, him will I bring into the land where he went; and his seed shall possess it. [Num.14:22-24]

God declared that Caleb had "another spirit with him." This is a clear statement concerning the root of the problem: the people were gripped by a different spirit from the spirit Caleb was obeying. God thus identified that He was responding to spiritual warfare among His people.

The reality of spiritual warfare is reflected in the acknowledgment by the heathen nations that Jehovah was the God of Israel. Those nations could not deny the existence of Jehovah because of the ever present question of who was the more powerful, their gods or Jehovah. The heathen nations believed the magicians had access to the power of the gods and that power was inherent in those who used incantations to confer with the gods. King Balak sent for Balaam, one of a family of magicians, seeking his aid:

> ...curse me this people, for they are too mighty for me, peradventure I shall prevail, that we may smite them, and that I may drive them out of the land: ... [Num. 22:6]

Balak was turning to spiritual warfare by seeking supernatural sources to place a curse of destruction upon God's people. God commanded Balaam not to go with Balak's men. Balaam vacillated between Balak's request for divination and serving Jehovah. Finally, God used a donkey to speak to Balaam, giving him permission to go but warned to speak only the words God would give him. Greedy Balaam tried several times to curse Israel but the power of God prevailed and Balaam spoke only God's blessings over Israel. Satan's power once again gave way to the greater power of God.

The death of Moses brought the mantle of spiritual warfare upon the shoulders of Joshua. He patiently waited for divine direction from Jehovah. When God's confirmation came, Joshua called the people to move forward again. Two men were sent to reconnoiter the land and the city of Jericho. Upon their return to Joshua, they reported: "Truly the Lord hath delivered into our hands all the land; for even all the inhabitants of the country do faint because of us." [Joshua 2:24] The mighty power of God over the power of darkness was about to be manifest. The ensuing spiritual warfare saw the Jordan crossed by God's people and the fall of the city of Jericho as the awesome power of God overcame that of the enemy. Yet in the utter destruction of Jericho, Satan's evil influence was evident as one man, Achan, took spoils from the city and brought the wrath of God down upon the children of Israel. Spiritual warfare never ceases.

Every battle fought by Joshua and God's people as they sought to possess the land was not only waged at the physical or human level, but also on a spiritual level in a supernatural conflict between God and the forces of evil. Time and space cannot be taken here but any serious person can find confirmation of that fact in the records of the Old Testament. The witness is most clear that God led His people in both physical warfare and in spiritual warfare.

The division of the land among the tribes of Israel was followed by spiritual decay among God's people. It is evident in the murmurings of the children of Joseph and their dissatisfaction over their portion of the land. This, together with their fear of the Canaanites, caused them to seek a different portion of land. They came in arrogance and pride to demand of Joshua a better choice of the land. The seeds of darkness are evident in the pride and tribal jealousy which eventually led to national decay - both physically and spiritually.

The entire period of the Judges saw the continuing work of darkness in the relationship between the people and God. The books of Samuel and Kings reveal the same conditions. The sin of idolatry throughout this period is a recurring theme. While it is true that the worship of Jehovah was maintained, it is also true that it was often combined with the heathen rites of adjoining nations. Baal worship flourished.

Judges 2:10-23 and Jeremiah 32:33-35 give vivid descriptions of this continuous return to idolatry by the Israelites. In the Judges passage there is a reference to Asteroth whose worship can be traced back directly to Semiiramis, the wife of Nimrod. The unbridled sexual licentiousness which made up an essential aspect of devotion to this goddess of fertility, because of its gross nature, must not be described here. The hand of Satan is evident in it all and he successfully turned the hearts of God's people again and again.

The account of Gideon demonstrates the reality of spiritual warfare waged throughout the period of the judges. An angel of God appeared to Gideon calling him to deliver Israel out of the hands of the Midianites. Gideon accepted the call and carried out the first part by throwing down his father's altar to Baal, cutting down the grove by it and building an altar to Jehovah God. When the people confronted the father of Gideon with the destruction of Baal's altar, he knew that God had manifested His power and said to the people:

> Will you plead for Baal? Will ye save him? He that will plead for him, let him be put to death while it is yet morning, and if he will be a god, let him plead for himself, because one has cast down his altar." [Judges 6:31]

In the battle which followed, God led Gideon and 300 men to victory over 135,000 Midianites. The selection of those 300 men is significant. Edersheim, in his Bible history, looked to the Jewish tradition for an explanation as to why those 300 men were chosen.

> If we ask about the rationale of these men's distinction, we conclude, of course, that it indicated the bravest, and most ardent warriors, who would not stoop to kneel, but

hastily quenched their thirst out of the hollow of their hand, in order to hasten to battle. But, Jewish tradition assigns another and deeper meaning to it. It declares that the practice of kneeling was characteristic of the service of Baal, and hence the kneeling down to drink when exhausted betrayed the habit of idolaters. Thus, the three hundred would represent those in the host of Israel -- "All the knees which have not bowed unto Baal.! (1 Kings 19:18)" [Edersheim, p. 138]

The deliverance wrought by this tremendous victory lasted only so long as Gideon lived. And so it was throughout that period of Israel's history.

The name of Baal repeatedly appears as the earthly representative of Satan's kingdom over against God's kingdom. The two kingdoms remain locked in spiritual warfare throughout the Old Testament record. A close friend of mine is in the midst of lengthy research into the role of Baal and Baal worship. The goal of that research is to clearly determine the effect of Baal worship as it interrelates with Christian worship. From the incomplete research a picture is already emerging of the influence of Baal worship upon literature, religion and the naming of cities and rulers throughout the world.

Idolatry, in general, and Baal worship accompanied by devotion to Ashteroth, in particular, continued to corrupt Israel throughout her history. However, this was not Satan's only method in his continuing effort to thwart God's purpose to establish a kingdom of righteousness on the earth. He would exploit every weakness of man to gain his end.

After Saul was made the first king in Israel, a flaw of character was soon demonstrated. Instead of patiently waiting for the high priest, Samuel, Saul offered sacrifices to God before entering into battle. Since he was not of the priesthood, he had drastically disobeyed the commandment of God. When Samuel arrived, he prophesied that God would establish another lineage on the throne of Israel:

But now thy kingdom shall not continue: the Lord hath sought him a man after his own heart, and the Lord hath commanded him to be captain over his people, because thou has not kept that which the Lord commanded thee. [1 Sam. 13:14]

Instead of repentance Saul allowed jealousy to flame in his heart.

Satan fanned that flame until fits of madness overtook Saul and he tried again and again to kill David, God's anointed servant. I am sure modern psychiatry would label Saul's condition as some form of insanity. However, the word of God says "an evil spirit from the Lord terrified him." (1 Sam. 16:14, alternate reading.)

Do not be misled into thinking because God sent the spirit it was not demonic. As we learn from Job and Peter's experience (Luke 22:31), Satan is continually seeking permission from God to take advantage of man's areas of vulnerability. Sometimes God grants permission.

David, the sweet psalm-singer of Israel, the man after God's own heart, was not immune from the onslaughts of Satan. His particular weakness was found in his sexual appetite. This weakness, as exploited by Satan, brought David to the point of becoming a thief, deceiver and murderer. (Remember, Satan is the father of lies and a murderer from the beginning.) David stole Bathsheba, the wife of Uriah; attempted to cover the resulting pregnancy by bringing Uriah home from the war; failing in this, he arranged for Uriah's death in battle.

It could be said that David's sins were far worse than Saul's. Why, then, was David not accorded greater punishment? The profound difference between these two men's spiritual character is David's repentant heart. When Nathan, the prophet, said to him, "thou art the man," David acknowledged his sin. When his son died as a punishment, David, as Job, "In all this... sinned not, nor charged God foolishly." (Job 1:22) Satan's best efforts are effectively overturned by acknowledging one's sin and repenting from the heart. Attempting to cover-up or blame others gives Satan opportunity to become entrenched in a person's life.

Even the godliness of David and the wisdom of Solomon failed to cleanse Israel of its proclivity to idolatry. The intensity of the spiritual warfare is clearly seen in the encounter between Elijah and the priests of Baal on Mt. Carmel. This was a test of power. The priests of Baal worshipped the powers of nature, whereas Elijah worshipped Jehovah God. The story is well known but let us turn to Edersheim's words:

> Now commenced a scene which baffles description. Ancient writers have left us accounts of the great Baal-Festivals, and they closely agree with the narrative of the Bible, only furnishing further details. First rose a comparatively moderate, though already wild cry to Baal; followed by a dance around the altar, beginning with a swinging motion to and fro. The howl then became

louder and louder, and the dance more frantic. They whirled round and round, ran wildly through each other's ranks, always keeping up a circular motion, the head low bent, so that their long dishevelled hair swept the ground. Ordinarily the madness now became infectious, and the onlookers joined in the frenzied dance. But Elijah knew how to prevent this. It was noon – and for hours they had kept up their wild rites. With cutting taunts and bitter irony, Elijah now reminded them that since Baal was Elohim, the fault must lie with them. He might be otherwise engaged, and they must cry louder – stung to madness, they became more frantic than before, and what we know as the second and third acts in these feasts ensued. The wild howl passed into piercing demonical yells. In their madness, the priests bit their arms and cut themselves with the two-edged swords which they carried and with lances – As blood began to flow, the frenzy reached its highest pitch. When first one, then others, commenced to 'prophesy,' moaned and groaned, then burst into rhapsodic cries, accusing themselves, or speaking to Baal, or uttering broken incoherent sentences. All the while they beat themselves with heavy scourges, loaded or armed with sharp points, and cut themselves with swords and lances – sometimes even mutilating themselves – since the blood of the priests was supposed to be specially propitiatory with Baal." [Edersheim, p. 17,18]

Can there be any doubt that this was spiritual warfare? Unable to summon the power of Baal, the priests and all present were to see the power of Jehovah flash from the heavens and consume the sacrifice and the very altar upon which it was offered. Once again, Israel was brought back into a covenant relationship with Jehovah - but the relationship was short-lived. The spiritual warfare is fierce between the kingdom of God and that of Satan. There is little time to celebrate a victory before the next battle begins.

The whole history of the two kingdoms of Israel and Judah is one of ongoing spiritual and physical warfare. A procession of righteous and evil kings appear in the holy record. The people vacillate between worship of Jehovah and worship of Baal. The altars and groves of Baal are destroyed and rebuilt over and over again as the people return to Jehovah and then fall back into the evil worship of Baal. Land is taken and lost again as the people endeavor to possess the land for Jehovah. Always the servants of Satan contend with God's people in the great effort to destroy God's kingdom on earth.

It would appear with the fall of Judah to Babylon that Satan had won the spiritual warfare which raged throughout the Old Testament era. The Davidic government was gone; the whole land lay in the possession of conquering enemies; the people were carried away into captivity and scattered to the far winds. But the words of Isaiah reminded the people that God's plan was yet to unfold:

> And it shall come to pass in the last days, that the mountain of the Lord's house shall be established in the top of the mountains, and shall be exalted above the hills; and all the nations shall flow unto it. And many people shall go and say, Come ye, and let us go up to the mountain of the Lord, to the house of the God of Jacob; and He will teach us of His ways, and we will walk in His paths: for out of Zion shall go forth the Law, and the word of the Lord from Jerusalem. [Isaiah 2:2,3]

The inability of God's people to possess and hold the land did not stop God's plan, nor did it herald the end of spiritual warfare. Nehemiah went before his king requesting permission to rebuild Jerusalem. Receiving approval of his request, he returned to the ruins of that city. When Sanballat and his followers heard of it, they became quite angry. The anger of Sanballat served the purposes of Satan since a rebuilt Jerusalem could not be allowed. If Jerusalem was to rise again from the ruins, God's plan would arise with it. Sanballat, with the others, devised a plan to stop there building:

> ... They shall not know, neither see, till we come into the midst among them, and slay them, and cause the work to cease." [Neh. 4:11]

Warned of the plan Nehemiah set into motion a plan of defense:

> Be not ye afraid of them; remember the Lord, which is great and terrible, and fight for your brethren, your sons, and your daughters, your wives, and your houses." [Neh. 4:14]

The will of Satan, when pitted against the plan of God, always places demands upon those involved. Spiritual warfare always requires physical sacrifice. Nehemiah reports:

And it came to pass, when our enemies heard that it was known unto us, and God had brought their counsel to nought, that we returned all of us to the wall, everyone unto his work. They which builded on the wall, and they that bare burdens, with those that laded, everyone with one of his hands wrought in the work, and with the other hand held a weapon. For the builders, everyone had his sword girded by his side, and so builded. And he that sounded the trumpet was by me." [Neh. 4:16,18]

And so the temple was built, Jerusalem restored and the nation of Israel re-established. Although the nation was not free of gentile domination, the worship of Jehovah as God was unfettered and the people of Jehovah were freed from idolatry. Never again were the Israelites, i.e. the Jews, to be involved in the worship of idols.

SPIRITUAL WARFARE
(N.T. Section)

The guerrilla tactics of Satan against God's people continued into an era unrecorded in the scriptures but adequately reported by the historians. Latourette in his HISTORY OF CHRISTIANITY summarizes the period following the rebuilding of Jerusalem:

A new temple was built at Jerusalem which became the centre not only for the Jewish population of that region, but also for thousands of Jews who were scattered in other parts of western Asia and of the Mediterranean Basin. The tie which held the Jews together was religious and the religion was Judaism. The loyalty of the Jews to their religion was heightened by persecution. Antiochus Epiphenes, one of the Seleucids who in succession to Alexander the Great built a realm in Syria and adjacent lands, sought to force Greek culture and manners on the Jews. This was met by a revolt led by the Maccabees and was followed by the setting up of a small state in which the high priest was the central figure. It also intensified among many the zeal for their faith. Later in the first century before Christ, the Jewish state was brought within the growing power of Rome. Herod, of non-Jewish stock, but married into the Maccabeean family, with the consent of Rome established himself over the little state and rebuilt the temple in Jerusalem. Here was a sad ending of the Maccabean dream. That dream had envisioned a community in which God's will as expressed in the Jewish law and prophets was to be perfectly observed. The outcome was a state governed by an alien ruler whose chief ambition was his own power and the establishment of a dynasty. Yet it was during the reign of Herod that Jesus was born and under Herod's descendants that Christianity had its inception." [Latoutette, pp. 10,11]

Up to this time Satan's efforts had been directed towards the destruction of God's chosen people. Failing in this he would corrupt them until their special identity could be eradicated. Satan had not yet succeeded in this but the Israelites had been reduced to a seemingly powerless remnant unable to influence the rest of the world in the worship of Jehovah. The stage was set for God's great redemptive act - an act defying human comprehension.

A child is conceived in a virgin woman's womb through the power of the Holy Spirit. Unable to stop or in any way hinder this mysterious act, Satan looked for the next possible opening for attack.

Satan easily found that opening in King Herod. Threatened by the report of the wise men concerning the new-born "king of the Jews," Herod sought some means to destroy him. Unable to find the child, he:

... sent forth, and slew all the children that were in Bethlehem, and in all the coasts thereof, from two years old and under, according to the time he had diligently inquired of the wise men. [Matt. 2:16]

Jesus was not among those slain. Joseph, warned by an angel, fled with Mary and Jesus into Egypt. This outburst of spiritual warfare exacted a terrible toll of innocent victims. Such is the way of all warfare.

Satan's next attack is lodged directly at Jesus in an attempt to force Him to take up His divine prerogatives, thereby denying and negating His true humanity. He first tempted Jesus (who had been fasting) to call upon His divinity and change the stones into bread. Failing there, Satan next tempts Jesus to test the Father's will to save Him should he leap from the pinnacles of the temple. Failing again, he tempts Jesus with all the kingdoms of the world. Satan was unable to get to Jesus through the needs of the body, the pride of life or the desires of the eyes.

64

Satan utterly failed in this attempt to stop God's plan of salvation and the establishment of His kingdom on earth. (See Matt. 4:1-11; Mark 1:12-15; Luke 4:1-13.)

Before Jesus was established in His own ministry, the last of the Old Testaments prophets burst upon Israel. The preaching of John, the Baptist, began to turn the people, now caught in the web of tradition and legalism, from outward observance to heart-held obedience. Repentance was his theme and water baptism was his practice. Hundreds, perhaps thousands, received his word gladly and were baptized, including the earliest disciples of Jesus.

Satan could not let this happen unchallenged. John's preaching reached the ears of the current Herod who, upon inquiry, was told that he was unlawfully living with his brother's wife. When Herod refused this opportunity to repent, he gave ground to Satan who was waiting for just such an opportunity. Sometime after having John thrown in prison, Herod held a party for a bunch of his political allies. He had Salome, his step-daughter, entertain by dancing for him and his friends - and Satan took control. Herod, overcome with drunkenness and lust, promised Salome anything she wanted, even to half of his kingdom. The young girl, not knowing what to do, ran to her mother for advice. Herodias, consumed with hatred and desiring revenge, told her to ask for the head of John, the Baptist. Salome returned to Herod with the request and because of pride and an unwillingness to back down in front of his friends, Herod ordered the crime to be done.

Look at the "works of the flesh" Herod made available to Satan by not repenting: drunkenness, lust, hatred, vengeance, pride and murder. (See Gal. 5) But Satan did not stop God's purposes. John "... the voice crying in the wilderness..." had already announced, "Behold the lamb of God which taketh away the sins of the world." And John's disciples began to follow Jesus.

With the advent of Jesus Christ a whole new concept of spiritual warfare was introduced. Until now, spiritual warfare had been conducted primarily through the physical battles between Israel and the nations around them. But in the ministry of Jesus Christ, every bondage placed upon man by Satan came under attack. Jesus spelled it out clearly in the synagogue of Nazareth:

> The spirit of the Lord is upon Me, because He hath anointed Me to preach the gospel to the poor; He hath

sent me to heal the brokenhearted, to preach deliverance to the captives, and recovering of sight to the blind, to set at liberty them that are bruised, to preach the acceptable year of the Lord. [Luke 4:18,19]

The gauntlet was thrown down - Satan's hold on mankind was challenged.

Every area of man's life under bondage to Satan was now a battlefield as Jesus Christ, anointed by the Holy Spirit, engaged the enemy in total spiritual warfare. Let it be clearly understood that every bondage placed upon man comes from Satan, not from God, and that Jesus Christ ministers freedom to break every bondage.

The open warfare began almost immediately as Satan responded to the challenge. First, doubt rose as Jesus spoke to the people of Nazareth. "Is not this Joseph's son," the villagers asked. As Jesus responded, wrath took control:

... (they) rose up, and thrust Him out of the city, and led Him unto the brow of the hill whereon their city was built, that they might cast Him down headlong. But he passing through the midst of them went His way. [Luke 4:29,30]

And so it was persecution at the hands of men (and those men His childhood neighbors and friends) began for Jesus Christ. Jesus was anointed not only with power, but with authority:

And in the synagogue (at Capernaum) there was a man, which had a spirit of an unclean devil, and cried out with a loud voice, saying, Let us alone; what have we to do with thee, thou Jesus of Nazareth? Art thou come to destroy us? I know thee who thou art; the Holy One of God. And Jesus rebuked him, saying Hold thy peace, and come out of him. And when the devil had thrown him in the midst of them, he came out of him, and hurt him not." [Luke 4:33-35]

It might be noted here by those who believe and teach that Jesus was not involved in violent deliverances that the man was thrown by the unclean spirit. That would seem to be somewhat violent!

This incident was followed very shortly by the healing of Peter's mother-in-law and others. And then "devils also came out of a man, crying out, and saying, Thou art Christ the Son of God." (Luke 4:41) The point I wish to establish is that the Satanic kingdom knew that open spiritual warfare was beginning.

The case of the Gadarene man, possessed with a legion of unclean spirits, reveals the reality of the spiritual warfare that raged wherever Jesus ministered. Scripture says that Jesus had commanded an unclean spirit to come out of the man. That spirit controlled the man's mind and body "for oftentimes it had caught him: and he was kept bound in chains and fetters; and he broke the bands, and was driven of the devil into the wilderness."

Note that the controlling spirit knew who was confronting him: "When he saw Jesus, he cried out, and fell down before Him, and with a loud voice said, What have I to do with thee, Jesus, thou Son of God most high? I beseech thee, torment me not." Likewise, the unclean spirits knew that the authority of the Most High God was with Jesus: "And they besought him that He would not command them to go out into the deep." With the departure of the unclean spirits, one would assume the spiritual warfare of that incident would cease. But just the opposite takes place. When the people came to see what had been done they pleaded with Jesus "to depart from them; for they were taken with great fear." (See Luke 8:26-36.)

Such is the nature of spiritual warfare, especially when there is a direct confrontation between the authority of the living God and the bondage of unclean spirits. What is so evident in this incident and others is how Satan uses fear as a tool to hinder the work of God's kingdom on earth. Fear grips those who do not understand and that serves Satan's purposes in spiritual warfare.

The religious leaders became an unknowing tool in the spiritual conflict between God's kingdom and Satan's. They demanded of Jesus: "Who is this which speaketh blasphemies? Who can forgive sins, but God alone?" (Luke 5:21) In their concept of righteousness, they unwittingly became involved in the spiritual warfare now gaining intensity because of Jesus' ministry.

> Ye Pharisees make clean the outside of the cup and the platter; but your inward part is full of ravening and wickedness. Ye (Scribes) have taken away the key of knowledge: ye entered not in yourselves, and them that were entering in ye hindered. (They) began to urge Him

vehemently, and to provoke Him to speak of many things: laying wait for Him, and seeking to catch something out of His mouth, that they might accuse Him. [Luke 11:37-54]

Before His death, Jesus warned His disciples that spiritual warfare would be waged against them also:

They shall put you out of the synagogues: yea, the time cometh, that whosoever killeth you will think that he doeth God service. [John 16:2]

We know that Paul was one of many who fulfilled those words of our Lord. The spiritual warfare reached a high point in the closing days of the ministry of Jesus. Our Lord spoke directly to it in the upper room:

Verily, verily I say unto you, that one of you shall betray me ... he it is to whom I shall give a sop, when I have dipped it.... and after (Jesus gave to Judas Iscariot) the sop Satan entered into him. [John 13:18-30]

The stage was now set for Satan's greatest attack upon God and His kingdom. If he could destroy Jesus, Satan apparently reasoned, God's plan and kingdom would come to nought. The spiritual warfare was building to its climatic point.

Satan struck quickly. A band of men came to the Garden of Gethsemane led by Judas who pointed out Jesus that He might be taken captive. After the arrest of Jesus, fear gripped Peter and he denied knowing his Lord. Jesus was brought before Pilate, who said he could find no fault in Him. But again fear reared its ugly head and Pilate, desiring to protect his position, said to the angry crowd: "Ye have a custom, that I should release unto you one at the passover: will ye therefore that I release unto you the King of the Jews?" Satan was to have his day and his evil influence burst forth in the crowd which cried: "not this man, but Barabbas." Again Pilate sought to release Jesus but the crowd cried out: "Away with him, away with him, crucify him." (See John 18.) Pilate delivered Jesus into the hands of the executioners to be crucified. Fear was making its inroads within the hearts and minds of the disciples as they all forsook Him and fled. Satan must have reasoned that he had finally stopped God's plan.

Satan apparently calculated that with Jesus dead and His disciples in despair the warfare was over and he had a free hand in the world.

He did not seem to realize (certainly no one else did, either) that the crucifixion cancelled sin's debt, that the surrection broke the power of sin's bondage and that God was about to fulfill His long-held intention to put the power and authority to wage spiritual warfare into the hands of men.

An early example of God's ultimate intention was demonstrated when Jesus commissioned the Twelve. Scripture tells us the disciples, including Judas Iscariot, were sent out with power over unclean spirits.

> ... they went out, and preached that men should repent.
> And they cast out many devils, and anointed with oil
> many that were sick, and healed them. [Mark 6:12,13]

What an example is set before those of us who witness and teach after the day of Pentecost when the Holy Spirit was poured out upon all flesh. These men - who were no different from other men who have lived upon the earth - went out with power preaching repentance, casting out devils, and healing the sick. They exercised authority and power over the enemy. Brothers and sisters, ought we not ask ourselves what we have done with the power of Pentecost?

Later, seventy disciples were sent out with the same authority and power. Returning, they cried out with joy, "Lord, even the devils are subject unto us through thy Name." Jesus responded, saying:

> ... I beheld Satan as lightning fall from heaven. Behold,
> I give unto you power to tread on serpents and scorpi-
> ons, and over all the power of the enemy; and nothing
> shall by any means hurt you. [Luke 10:18-19]

The placing of spiritual warfare into men's hands was not limited to the twelve or the seventy. It has been placed into the hands of all believers. Our Lord and Savior speaks to all believers just as He spoke to His disciples. In the Gospel of John, Jesus says:

> Verily, verily, I say unto you, he that believeth on me, the
> works that I do shall he do also; and greater works than
> these shall he do; because I go unto my Father. [John
> 14:12]

Some believers have lost sight of this commissioning or else they do not grasp its significance. I say this on the basis of our Lord's work, as a man, recorded in scripture and which work is not evidenced in the lives of most believers. There is no indication in God's word that Jesus placed this promise within a time frame excluding our day and age. The only qualifying statement that may be found in His words is "he that believeth on me." It would seem rather clear that all believers from that day to this are to do the works which Jesus did in His public ministry.

All believers have the promise of our Lord that they need not go into spiritual warfare without being empowered.

> And I will pray the Father, and He shall give you another Comforter, that he may abide with you forever; even the Spirit of truth; ... (which) is the Holy Ghost, whom the Father will send in my name, He shall teach you all things, and bring all things to your remembrance, whatsoever I have said unto you. [John 14:16,17,26]

The Greek text of this passage indicates that the word translated "Comforter" is to be understood in the context of an "Intercessor." It is taken from the word parakletos which carries the meaning of someone called to another's aid. In John 14:16, it is used to identify the Holy Spirit as the helper or intercessor who comes to be with and dwell within those whom Jesus Christ, the Intercessor, has called and commissioned. The warfare rests in the hands of all believers.

Christ's disciples received that empowering on the day of Pentecost and took up the ministry started by Jesus. There is clear evidence of the Holy Spirit's empowering in the preaching of Peter in the second chapter of Acts. Peter called the people to repentance and three thousand people accepted the message of salvation immediately and others were added daily.

Signs and wonders occurred as the Apostles ministered. A lame man asking alms heard Peter say:

> Silver and gold have I none; but such as I have give I thee: In the name of Jesus Christ of Nazareth rise up and walk.... And he leaping up stood, and walked, and entered with them into the temple, walking, and leaping and praising God. [Acts 3:6,7]

A whole new phase of warfare now began as men took the offensive against the bondages which had hindered and tormented mankind. No longer was the offensive waged by one man, Jesus. Now all believers were to be involved.

The healing of the lame man confronted the religious leaders with a great problem. They could not deny the healing and their position of religious leadership was threatened. Spiritual warfare had now come to their doorstep. A simple solution was sought: command these men to stop preaching and performing signs and wonders in the name of Jesus. It would have been easier to have stopped wild horses from running than to stop these men filled with the Holy Spirit.

We who live and witness in an environment of safety should look at the example of these people of God and note their boldness. When Peter and John reported back to their group, a worship and praise session began. They prayed:

> And now, Lord, behold their threatenings: and grant unto thy servants, that with all boldness they may speak thy word, by stretching forth thine hand to heal; and that signs and wonders may be done by the name of thy Holy Child Jesus. And when they had prayed, the place was shaken where they were assembled together; and they were all filled with the Holy Ghost, and they spoke the word of God with boldness. [Acts 4:29-31]

This day and age of Christianity could surely use some shaking by the Holy Spirit and boldness to confront the enemy. We need boldness that dares ask for signs and wonders even though the calm waters of present day Christianity might be rippled.

There was a bond of unity which drew the followers of Jesus Christ into a communal sharing of possessions but this did not prevent the enticement of evil playing upon men's minds. Ananias and Sapphira kept back part of their possessions and claimed to give all of it. Peter's response went to the very heart of the problem: "... Why hath Satan filled thine heart to lie to the Holy Ghost...? Thou hast not lied unto men but unto God." [Acts 5:3] Ananias and Sapphira became casualties of spiritual warfare. The several participants in this one event - Satan, the Holy Spirit, Ananias, Sapphira, and Peter - demonstrated that this was truly a confrontation between the forces of light and darkness for control of men's minds and lives. Let no one be confused as to who triumphed in this encounter. The swift judgement of God brought a healthy fear upon the Church.

The Apostles continued to preach with signs and wonders accompanying their witness. The sick were laid out on the streets in order that Peter's shadow might fall on them and healings occurred. Multitudes came from all directions around Jerusalem, bringing the sick and those with unclean spirits and all were healed.

The enemy could not allow this to continue. Too much notoriety was being gained by these people of God. The pride of the religious leaders was touched and the Bible says they were "... filled with indignation and laid their hands on the Apostles, and put them in the common prison." We see the evidence of spiritual warfare being waged openly as God responded by sending an angel who "... opened the prison doors and brought them forth, and said, Go, stand, speak in the temple to the people all the words of this life." (See Acts 5:18-20.)

The Apostles did as they were told by God and again were brought before the high priest, the captain of the temple, and the chief priests. When asked why they continued to preach and perform signs and wonders, Peter's response again went to the heart of the matter. The evil minds of men killed Jesus whom God has raised to be a Prince and Savior "... to give repentance to Israel and forgiveness of sins. And we are His witnesses of these things; and so is also the Holy Ghost, whom God hath given to them that obey Him." The evil minds of the counsel sought but one solution - KILL THEM. (See Acts 5:29-33.)

One man, a Pharisee, recognized there might be deeper implications in this whole matter than appeared on the surface. He laid before the council the possibility that they were participants in spiritual warfare and for a moment of time the attack of the enemy was blunted.

> ... Refrain from these men, and let them alone: for if this counsel or this work be of men, it will come to nought: but if it be of God ye cannot overthrow it; lest haply ye be found even to fight against God. And to him they agreed: and when they had called the apostles, and beaten them, they commanded that they should not speak in the name of Jesus, and let them go. [Acts 5:38-40]

Stephen was a man of great faith and performed wonders and miracles among the people. This brought a challenge from some in the synagogue. When the leaders of the synagogue found they lacked the wisdom to dispute with Stephen they brought false accusations against him. The evil influence upon their minds was so powerful they were able to stir up the people, the elders and the scribes who brought him before the council. Once again, the battle lines of spiritual warfare were drawn for all to see. He was accused of having said "... that this Jesus of Nazareth

72

shall destroy this place, and shall change the customs which Moses delivered us." When questioned, Stephen responded with a review of the history of Israel and the evil influence recorded in that account. Fury rose in the hearts of those who heard and they took him out of the city, stoned him and cast his clothing at the feet of Saul. Satan must have been overjoyed. A battle had been won and now another man, named Saul, would be used for his evil purposes. (See Acts 6.)

Saul served the purposes of Satan well.

> ... he made havoc of the church, entering into every house, and haling men and women committed them to prisons. [Acts 8:3]

His efforts scattered the followers of Jesus throughout the Roman Empire. Not satisfied with his destructive work in one locality:

> ... Saul, yet breathing out threatenings and slaughter against the disciples of the Lord, went unto the high priest, and desired of him letters to Damascus to the synagogues, that if he found any of this way, whether they were men or women, he might bring them bound unto Jerusalem. [Acts 9:1,2]

The journey to Damascus became the setting for spiritual battle when light confronted darkness and darkness gave way. As Paul traveled that road:

> ... suddenly there shined round about him a light from heaven: and he fell to the earth, and heard a voice saying unto him, Saul, Saul, why persecutest thou me? [Acts 9:3,4]

So Satan's seeming victory at the stoning of Stephen was short-lived and ultimately served God's purposes. Out of the encounter on the road to Damascus, God raised a mighty warrior to do battle for the Lord Jesus Christ. In time his endeavors would establish churches throughout the northern rim of the Mediterranean Sea.

Paul's ministry was one of constant spiritual warfare as mighty works of power accompanied his witness. A young woman possessed of a spirit of divination followed after Paul until he:

> ... turned and said to the spirit, I command thee in the

73

name of Jesus Christ to come out of her. And he came out the same hour. [Acts 16:18]

Because they cast out the spirit of divination, Paul and Silas were beaten and thrown into prison. At midnight, in the midst of a worship and praise session by Paul and Silas, an earthquake shook the prison, opening its doors and breaking the shackles of the prisoners. This unusual series of events must be acknowledged as a spiritual confrontation between the forces of light and darkness. And again, darkness gave way before the light. The jailer was converted and, with his family, became the basis for a powerful witness in Philippi that established one of the strongest churches in the area.

This was typical of Paul's work. He would preach and perform mighty works and men under Satan's evil influence would attempt to thwart his efforts, even to kill him, if possible. The result would be the establishing of a church to continue the witness to Christ's death and resurrection. And so it should be today. Perhaps we would not always face death but our work and witness should still be accompanied by the powerful operation of the Holy Spirit, overcoming Satan and establishing the Church.

The sin principle loosed in mankind at the time of Adam's fall constantly challenged the work of Paul. His witness of the gospel of Jesus Christ resulted in warfare between the kingdom of light and the kingdom of darkness. Incident after incident is recorded showing the intensity of the spiritual warfare which arose wherever Paul traveled and ministered. At Thessalonica:

> ... the Jews which believed not, moved with envy, took unto them certain lewd fellows of a baser sort, and gathered a company, and set all the city on an uproar, and assaulted the house of Jason to bring them out to the people. [Acts 17:5]

This same thing happened at Berea (Acts 17:13,) Corinth (Acts 18:12) and again at Ephesus (Acts 19.) Paul's encounter with the silversmith at Ephesus stands as clear evidence that this was more than a clash of human minds. The silversmith's livelihood depended upon the crafting of pagan idols. Paul caused the market to be depressed by teaching that the kingdom of God was at hand. The works of healing and deliverance which followed his teaching devastated the market for silver idols.

However, this was much deeper than an economical crises for the silversmiths. Demitrius called them together and said:

> ... this Paul hath persuaded and turned away much people, saying that they be no gods, which are made with hands: so that not only this our craft is in danger to be set at naught; but also that the temple of the great goddess Diana should be despised, and her magnificence should be destroyed, whom all Asia and the world worshippeth. [Acts 19:26,27]

While it is true that the town clerk was able to quiet down the crowd by pointing out that the worship of Diana was not necessarily the concern of the silversmiths and that Rome would intervene if there was a riot, this was actually a clash between the kingdom of light and that of darkness. It is also true in our own day that whenever light penetrates into the darkness - whether it be in economical, political or personal affairs, the elements of spiritual warfare emerge - the influence of evil comes to the surface and conflict ensues.

Many believe and teach that the miraculous ended with the passing of the Apostles. If such were true it could be readily agreed that the rebellion of Lucifer had been finally overcome and he, with his legions, had been bound and unable to act. Again, if this were the case, it would seem likely that in their writings and instructions to the churches these same Apostles would not have bothered to warn believers concerning a vanquished enemy. Perhaps most seriously, this view calls the doctrine of inspiration into question. If the miraculous were to end and Satan's efforts to cease, it is likely the Holy Spirit would have said something about it to the future church through the writings of the Apostles. However, quite the contrary is true.

Paul's language in Ephesians 6:10-18 is graphic and pointed - the enemy with which the Church was to do battle was not flesh and blood but that ancient foe of God called the devil. "Stand against the devil's schemes; struggle against the rulers, authorities, powers of this dark world, spiritual forces of evil in heavenly realms; extinguish flaming arrows of the evil one "are all fighting terms concerning an enemy that was then and is still destructive and implacable.

Again, in the same letter in which he speaks of his impending death, Paul warns Timothy not to quarrel with those in the church who oppose him. Rather, Timothy was to instruct them in the hope that "...they will come to their senses and escape from the trap of the devil who has taken them captive to do his will." [2 Tim. 2:26 NIV] So we see that at the very end of Paul's life and ministry the devil is actively attempting to snare believers and Paul is teaching to counteract the devil's strategy even after he is gone.

James wrote that believers are to "Resist the devil and he will flee from you." [James 4:7 NIV] Peter calls the devil "your enemy" and warns believers to "...resist him, standing firm in the faith." [1 Peter 5:8,9 NIV] John, the last of the Apostles, instructs that Jesus "...appeared to destroy the devil's work." Then he tells us how to discern between children of God and children of the devil. [1 John 3:7-10 NIV]

If the resurrection of Jesus from the dead brought to an end the works of the devil, how is it that there are still "children of the devil" to be reckoned with? It is obvious that the devil was still very much about his wicked business some 40-50 years after the resurrection.

Finally, there is the book of the Revelation. John, now in his nineties, is given a revelation of "...what is now and what will take place later." [Rev. 1:19 NIV] Throughout this book the devil is shown not only as an ultimately defeated foe but as one who continues to battle against God and His Church until, at last, he is cast into the Lake of Fire.

Take note of the language: (All quotations are from Revelation, NIV.)

...the devil will put some of you in prison... [2:10]

...they did not stop worshiping demons, ... Nor did they repent of their murders, their magic arts, their sexual immoralities, or their thefts. [9:20,21]

And there was war in heaven. Michael and his angels fought against the dragon ... that ancient serpent called the devil or Satan, who leads the whole world astray. [12:7-10]

But woe to the earth and the sea, because the devil has gone down to you! He is filled with fury, because he knows his time is short. [12:12]

Then the dragon was enraged ... and went off to make war against... those who obey God's commandments and hold to the testimony of Jesus. [12:17]

They are spirits of demons performing miraculous signs, and they go out to the kings of the whole world, to gather them for the battle on the great day of God Almighty. [16:14]

Regardless of the eschatalogy one holds, it must be agreed that the language of the Revelation portrays a constant continuous warfare on Satan's part against God and against God's people. Although his efforts are unabating, it is beyond question that Satan cannot prevail. The battles are fierce and frightening but the victory is assured. We shall overcome by the blood of the Lamb and word of our testimony.

I am convinced the attitude of many in Christendom is to seek calm waters. To speak of spiritual warfare stirs fear in the hearts of God's people, causing ripples to appear and might even roil the waters of the modern Christian church. If spiritual warfare can be limited to an occasional conversion of souls and the building of large edifices for that purpose, then little disturbance ensues and peace is maintained. But it is a pseudo peace, leaving Satan great territory in which to work his will unopposed. In our relationship with God and other believers, we are called to peace but concerning Satan and his hordes, God has not called believers to peace but to war and has thoroughly equipped them to do battle.

PART III: (PRACTICAL)

CHAPTER 3

REALITY OF UNCLEAN SPIRITS TODAY

Teaching and sharing in churches and other public meetings it has been my experience to find a general acceptance or, at least, an acknowledgment that some sort of Satanic personality exists. While there are those who teach that all evil works are personified under the name of Satan (tending to make Satan a figment of the imagination,) there does seem to be a general consensus that Satan does exist.

Most Christians, apparently, accept the description of Satan as presented in scripture but many have a problem when the subject of unclean spirits is discussed. The whole matter concerning the reality and work of unclean spirits or demons in our day seems difficult for them to comprehend. For many there is little desire or interest to even give the matter any serious thought. There seems to be a prevailing mind-set that if one does not give credence to the existence of the demonic, it all will go away.

It is important that no glory be given to the satanic kingdom and it is equally important that fear not be struck in the hearts of God's people. However, the reality of unclean spirits has been cunningly hidden by Satan behind the fear of many Christian leaders to speak out on this subject. Now this blanket of fear and apathy shrouds the churches and the work of the satanic forces in the lives of individuals is not recognized. This apathy has given Satan the freedom to ravage God's people at will with little or no response from the churches. This freedom is implied in the words of our Lord Jesus Christ:

> When the unclean spirit is gone out of a man, he walketh through dry places, seeking rest; and finding none, he saith, I will return unto my house whence I came out. And when he cometh, he findeth it swept and garnished. Then goeth he, and taketh to him seven other spirits more wicked then himself; and they enter in, and dwell there: and the last state of that man is worse than the first. [Luke 11:24-26]

These words are sufficient to keep many Christian leaders from even investigating the validity of inner-healing and deliverance. The words "and the last state is worse than the first" strike fear into their hearts. After all, no person wants to be responsible for causing another person to fall into a condition that is worse than when they first received ministry. In the light of this, it is thought more prudent to avoid the whole issue rather than risk worsening a situation.

Jesus' words were not spoken to strike fear into believers but to set forth the truth that the demonic kingdom is real and is capable of wreaking havoc. They are somber words of warning that serve to remind us that the deliverance ministry is not some light parlor game. The very life and personality of the afflicted is involved and is never to be taken lightly. However, the knowledgeable Christian worker knows his or her position as a child of God and that "... greater is He that is in you, than he that is in the world" (1 John 4:4.) Caution is in order but fear should never be allowed to deny anyone freedom from vexing satanic bondage.

In Luke 11 the Lord Jesus said that the unclean spirit had gone out of the person. Nothing is said as to why the spirit left. In my experience there have been several reasons why demons leave their habitation. Occasionally they leave on their own accord or, perhaps, on orders from a superior. Frequently, unclean spirits leave when a person is converted and, especially, when baptized with the Holy Spirit. In Jesus time on earth, it was most likely because the spirit was cast out in a deliverance session. In any event, something happened leaving an area in the man empty and clean. That area had been occupied by an unclean spirit. It had not left the man but had "gone out," indicating it had been inside of him.

This is not the end of the matter, however, for Jesus says that outside of a body the unclean spirit is unable to find rest. He travels about, seeking such a place. (What a description this is of being outside the fellowship of the living God! There is absolutely no rest for anyone outside of that relationship.) The unclean spirit returns to that person from whom he has departed and finds that the place he once inhabited is now swept and garnished (i.e. put in order.) Our Lord says the unclean spirit then calls in seven more who are more wicked than himself and they all move in.

If you are instrumental in causing an unclean spirit or spirits to leave a person, it is imperative that the empty spot in that person be filled with the things of God. Otherwise, that person may be in a potentially worse state than before! I have seen people leading others through the "sinner's prayer" without bringing that person to a commitment to the lordship of Jesus Christ. Without such a commitment that person is left vulnerable to satanic attack. In addition, there is often little or no follow-up to assure that if unclean spirits have left, the person will remain free. The newly liberated person must be taught how to stay free. It appears that our Lord felt it important to point out that once an unclean spirit has left a body, that body must be filled with something that will keep unclean spirits from re-entering or the person will not remain free.

Jesus has used a very common example to illustrate a vital point in remaining free of unclean spirits. We all understand that when renters leave a house, the landlord usually goes through the place cleaning, repairing, painting and doing whatever is needed to prepare for the next tenants. It is the landlord's intention to have new renters as soon as possible. An unoccupied house rapidly deteriorates and, it has been known, becomes an open invitation for freeloaders to occupy and vandals to destroy. So it is in the spirit realm.

When the unclean spirit is evicted (it seldom leaves of its own accord) a person readies his life for constant occupancy by the Holy Spirit through the word of God, prayer, fellowship of the saints and Christian service. By being filled continually with the Holy Spirit, this person will have available the gifts of the Spirit and the whole armour of God so that Satan and his demons can be successfully resisted. Should the maintenance of the spiritual life be neglected, this person will become vulnerable to demonic activity and, especially, by the very same unclean spirit that was originally cast out. It will return and bring others more wicked.

I believe this text sets forth a very basic truth which must be understood by all believers: whatever causes an unclean spirit to leave, that experience is not sufficient to prevent the return of the unclean spirit. In fact, the person becomes a more desirable place for the unclean spirit and its cohorts to inhabit. In this light, it is most important for a person, newly converted or who has just experienced the baptism with the Holy Spirit or who has just gone through deliverance to be instructed and helped to walk in those things that will keep a believer free of such undesirable tenants.

I am often questioned in workshops and seminars, "What is a demon?" There is no absolute answer to that question. I am personally persuaded that devils, demons and unclean spirits are that third of the angelic host which followed after Satan, forsaking their first estate, as recorded in Jude 6.

There may be those who would question the ability of unclean spirits to function when they are in everlasting chains awaiting the judgment day. The literal translation of the Jude passage indicates that the rebellious angels gave up their position of honor in God's heavenly place of habitation and are now under everlasting bonds of gloom until the day of judgment. There does not seem to be any indication that they are bound in such a way as to be restricted to a given location other than earth. Rather, the binding seems to be one of condition. I believe this is what was meant when an unclean spirit cried out to our Lord asking if He was moving their judgement ahead of its appointed time (Mt. 8:29.)

There is a teaching, based upon the Hebrew account of Genesis, which postulates that in the years before the flood there were men upon the earth who were the progeny of unnatural conceptions. This is deduced from the meaning of the word "Nephilim." Merrill Unger speaks of this word in this way:

> The form of the Hebrew word denotes a plural verbal or noun of passive significance, certainly from naphal, 'to fall,' so that the connotation is 'the fallen ones,' clearly meaning the unnatural offspring which were in the earth in the years before the flood, and also after that (Num. 13:33) when the sons of God came in unto the daughters of men (Gen.6:4.) [Unger's Dictionary, p. 402]

Unger then goes on to suggest that the giants spoken of were the result of mixed human and angelic birth.

It has been suggested to me by some who have been greatly influenced by this teaching that it is possible demons are the progeny of fallen angels. They draw this possibility from the words of Jude and Genesis 6:4. These passages are then understood in the context that the fallen angels were guilty of the same sins as the people of Sodom and Gomorrah and are capable of not only producing giants but also evil spirits to torment mankind. I find this difficult to accept because of the limited biblical evidence supporting such doctrines.

I teach, on the basis of scriptural evidence and personal experience, that demons, devils or unclean spirits are beings with personalities. They are spirits without bodies. I find myself in the position of being willing to accept the reality of an angelic host (which scripture details as ministering spirits sent to minister to the heirs of salvation, Heb. 1:13,14) I must, also, accept the reality that the fallen third of that angelic host still exists and functions on earth. Therefore, I am persuaded that demons are evil entities, without bodies, capable of entering and leaving a body and are, most likely, fallen angels. I desire to remain teachable in this but until shown clear scriptural evidence to the contrary, I feel this must be my position as to the identity and make-up of evil spirits.

The Bible makes no attempt to prove the existence of demons. It acknowledges their presence in the same way that it acknowledges the existence of God. The focus of scripture is upon the function of evil spirits, especially in reaction against God's love for His creation.

Satan does not possess the attributes of omniscience, omnipresence or omnipotence. One may then question how he maintains control over the whole earth. That control over men, women and the whole of creation can only be maintained through subordinates whom scripture identifies as devils, demons and unclean spirits. There is little doubt in my mind, on the basis of practical experience in confronting the hosts of hell in deliverance sessions, that global communication is not out of the realm of possibility for the satanic kingdom. Through such a global communication system and the authoritarian structure of the satanic kingdom, Satan is able to hold the whole world in darkness.

It is evident from scripture that the people of Jesus' day understood the reality of demonic forces and their work. This is clear in the accusation hurled at Jesus that He cast out demons by the power of Beelzebub. His response was "... if I by Beelzebub cast out devils, by whom do your children cast them out?" [Matt. 12:27] It is obvious that their "children" were dealing with demonic spirits.

Jesus confronted the unclean spirits within men, women and children and commanded them out with the authority granted Him by the heavenly Father - and they left. The reality of the unclean spirits was never questioned by the people nor by our Lord. He did little, if any, teaching concerning their reality instead He concentrated on dealing with them.

> And He was casting out a devil, and it was dumb. And
> it came to pass, when the devil was gone out, the dumb
> spake, and the people wondered. [Luke 11:14]

Certain facts standout rather clearly in this passage:

    1.) there was a demonic entity
       present;

    2.) the work manifested by that spirit
       was the prevention of speech;

3.) the demonic entity was inside the person since the passage says it came out;

4.) when the spirit departed the ability to speak was the immediate result.

While it is not clearly shown, the passage seems to indicate there was a passage of time between the command to leave and the actual departure of the unclean spirit. This may suggest that the unclean spirit resisted Jesus just as they often resist the servants of Jesus.

> Lord, have mercy on my son; for he is lunatic, and sore vexed; for often times he falleth into the fire, and oft into the water... And Jesus rebuked the devil: and he departed out of him: and the child was cured from that very hour. [Matt. 17:15-18]

Now, let us see the facts of this case:

1.) the boy was mentally disoriented;

2.) he was "vexed;" (Greek = harassment, weariness suffering, etc.)

3.) he often lost control of his body.

I am sure that a present day physician would diagnose this ailment as epilepsy. Jesus spoke with authority commanding the spirit to come out of the child; the spirit left and the boy was healed that same hour. That same authority was manifested in response to a concerned mother. The cry of a concerned mother:

> ... a woman of Canaan came ... and cried unto him, saying, Have mercy upon me, O Lord, thou Son of David; my daughter is grievously vexed with a devil, ... O Woman, great is thy faith: be it unto thee, even as thou wilt. And her daughter was made whole from that very hour. [Matt. 15:22-28]

Again certain facts stand out:

1.) the girl was tormented by a demonic being;

2.) Jesus tested the faith of the mother;

3.) because of the mother's faith, the girl
was delivered and healed.

The girl's problem was not psychological, as many would diagnose today; she was tormented by an unclean spirit and the casting out of that spirit brought healing. Some in today's churches have a difficult time accepting the reality of this happening in the modern world. Because of that reluctance many troubled people are taught to cope with the problem rather than to be healed.

Demonic torment is not just short-term, that is, like a little dart hitting now and then. It can be, and often is, quite long-term.

> And, behold, there was a woman which had a spirit of infirmity eighteen years, and was bowed together, and could in no wise lift up herself. And when Jesus saw her, he called her to him, and said unto her, Woman, thou art loosed from thine infirmity. And he laid his hands on her: and immediately she was made straight, and glorified God. And the ruler of the synagogue [was indignant] because that Jesus had healed on the sabbath day, ... The Lord then answered him, and said, ... And ought not this woman, being a daughter of Abraham, whom Satan hath bound, lo, these eighteen years, be loosed from this bond on the sabbath day? [Luke 13:11-16]

Now lest someone be moved to think that the spirit of infirmity mentioned here was an attitude rather than a demonic entity, note the source of her problem as identified by Jesus: "... whom Satan hath bound ..." Further, this case seems to be a direct confrontation between a satanic spirit and the Lord Jesus. No one, not even the woman herself, asked for her healing. Jesus called her to Himself and set her free. The woman was healed and glorified God.

We often see people in our ministry who are healed and set free of demonic activity but will not return to glorify God by witnessing to their deliverance in their home church. They fear what the leaders will say and do. Our ministry is thus labeled a para-church ministry because it is, for the most part and by necessity, conducted outside of church buildings. It would appear that Jesus had somewhat the same problem for, in this account, He violated synagogue procedure by healing on the sabbath and incurred the displeasure of the leaders.

Interestingly, the ruler of the synagogue seemed to have some knowledge of the practice of divine healing since his only complaint was that Jesus healed on the sabbath when there were the other six days of the week to do the work. It is also interesting that in this account Jesus laid His hands upon the woman and she was healed. There are those who teach that one should never lay hands on people to release them from demonic bondage - but Jesus did.

Since there is sufficient evidence that unclean spirits existed and were at work at the time of Jesus' personal ministry, this raises another issue that the Church urgently needs to face today. There must be clarity as to whether or not those same spirits exist today and are still at work. I have sought carefully in the biblical accounts for some clear evidence that unclean spirits were a phenomena only of those days. I have not been able to locate any evidence to support that view.

As a young man preparing for my confirmation, I once asked my pastor about the signs and wonders recorded in the New Testament. I even suggested that if they occurred in the days of Jesus, ought they not to still be occurring? I was advised that the signs and wonders which accompanied Christ's ministry occurred because he was God and that signs and wonders followed the ministry of the early leaders of the Church for two reasons: firstly, these men were trained by Him or had a direct commission to perform them; secondly, signs and wonders were needed to establish the Church because of the pagan practices and the use of magical power by those who opposed the gospel. In my youth, one did not question a pastor since his words were the equivalent of God's.

In seminary, several years later, I found that this same view still held and that to ripple the waters in this matter might throw doubt upon one's graduation and ordination. I do not know if that attitude still prevails; I pray it does not. I do know that many ministers, not only of that denomination but of others also, seem to hold similar views.

My search of scripture has led me to the conviction that no time is given for the cessation of demonic activity until Christ returns and the fulfillment of the judgment hovering over the satanic realm is accomplished. I find no indication the activities of unclean spirits were to be limited to the times of the early Church. There is nothing which says that only the superstition-ridden Medieval Church would be afflicted with a demon problem. Nor is there any reference that the Church would become so pure, righteous and sophisticated that demons would not dare manifest themselves.

God says, in the Old Testament, that His people are destroyed for lack of knowledge (Hosea 4:6) and it is my conviction those words speak also to the Church of our day. John 14:12 rather clearly states that believers in all ages are to carry out Christ's ministry, which includes spiritual warfare. It is time for war!

Yes - unclean spirits exist today; yes - they still indwell men, women and children; yes - they seek to steal, kill and destroy just as they did in Jesus' day. I do not say that to frighten anyone but I surely say it to smash at the apathy which grips the leaders of churches, great and small, in the world today. Satan is subject to the authority of Jesus Christ and the power of His shed blood. However, that authority and power is ineffectual if there is a lack of knowledge concerning its application and use. Christ's authority and power is not a security blanket behind which the Christian hides and lives out a fantasy in which demonic activity does not exist.

I have seen, with my own eyes, the result of unclean spirits functioning in men, women and children. I have seen how they are able to wrench and contort a human body. I have heard them speak using the speech faculties of the one they indwell. They have threatened, cursed and discredited Shirley and me. They have caused the person they indwelt to strike us, spit on us and in other ways attempt bodily harm against us. Praise God, He has led us into the knowledge of how to control such violence. It is because of what we have seen and experienced that this book has been written. It has been written in the hope that the Church will come to see the reality of spiritual warfare.

It is true - Satan and his subordinates are defeated. Their defeat came at the cross and was guaranteed by the resurrection of Jesus from the dead. But every believer must appropriate the necessary knowledge to initiate the victory of the Cross for himself, his family and others in the kingdom of God.

I have attempted in this part of the book to examine the Scriptural records in a rather cursory manner to determine if the spiritual warfare begun in heaven has continued through the ages to our day and time. It is most evident that the "sin principle "(introduced by Satan in the fall of the first man) has enticed and stirred the hearts and minds of men and women throughout the Old Testament record. While it is true, that God has dealt with man because of his rebellious nature, it must never be overlooked that the enemy has cleverly enticed men into serving his purposes. The fall of our first parents, the flood, the rise to power of Nimrod with the introduction of Baal worship, the physical warfare in the promised land, and the final fall of the two kingdoms of Israel and Judah all point back to the rebellion of Lucifer and his hatred of God. It would seem that an unbroken thread of spiritual warfare winds its way through the Old Testament record.

That same thread winds its way throughout the New Testament record as well. Beginning with the birth of Christ, the temptation, His ministry and, finally, the crucifixion all demonstrate Satan's unceasing efforts to thwart the purposes of God. The early Church was soon engaged in the relentless warfare. The Apostles warned and taught in strong language that the warfare would continue to the return of our Lord Jesus Christ.

So we see that the testimony of Scripture is consistent: Satan is the relentless foe of God from the beginning and continues his attacks in the present day. In the inner-healing/deliverance ministry we see a continuous flow of victims of spiritual warfare - torn and bound in mind and body - which further attests to Satan's unceasing activity.

The record of this truth is there for all to see. To limit spiritual warfare to only the conversion of souls, as many in modern Christianity are prone to do, serves as a dangerous cover-up of the reality of the warfare being waged continuously by the satanic kingdom. The desperate people finding help in this ministry often ask the same questions: "Why has the Church neglected this part of the ministry? Why are Church leaders so frightened of spiritual warfare?"

It is not my intent to try to answer for the Church. Rather, it is my heart's desire, by the help of God, to call the Church back to the reality that it is time for war. The enemy has run rough-shod over God's people but we are not helpless. We have been equipped with mighty weapons. We must learn to use them skillfully and, under the leadership of the Lord Jesus Christ, enter into this warfare. Now is the time for warfare against the forces of hell which have been loosed to prey upon God's people. I call upon all believers to put on your armour, lift up your shield and take up the sword. It is time for war!

CHAPTER 4

SPIRITUAL WARFARE TODAY

It is incongruous to believe spiritual warfare stopped with the demise of the Apostles and the evangelists of the early church. Yet, from my research and observation of current church practices, it would seem the general attitude of today's churches reflects such a conclusion. As I travel I see, in the churches, a tragic apathy toward an enemy who has not yet conceded defeat. Leaders and laity seem to be afraid to even consider the possibility that a state of warfare exists between Christians and Satan, and, at this very moment, may be exacting a toll in any given church - even your's.

The Church, through evangelism, is engaged in a spiritual battle to wrest souls away from the satanic camp. This is the first and foremost calling of the Church. Satan strikes back, wounding God's people, but who takes responsibility for the casualties of such spiritual warfare?

It is tragic that very few seminaries concern themselves with basic teachings about spiritual warfare. My three years of seminary classes and subsequent year of practical training touched very little upon the reality of unclean spirits. There was an acknowledgement that unclean spirits might work in the unregenerate and then, probably, only in the pagan parts of the world - certainly not in Christians. Yet, that same denomination sends men and women into those pagan lands without sufficient knowledge or training to deal with the attacks which unclean spirits may launch against them.

I came into the parish ministry with the fuzzy concept that I need only concern myself with the problems created by people's old nature and thought this was the sum and substance of their spiritual problems. But I soon came to realize men and women of God were suffering from problems that transcended the work of the old nature. Whenever compulsive behavior of any kind was encountered, my training was to send the person to a qualified professional. I, ordained to serve the Most High God, could not be expected to deal with such complex problems.

How ill-prepared I was on that fateful night when I was called out to minister to a young Christian man under satanic control. How I wished someone had taken the responsibility to train me in confronting the reality of the demonic realm. If the denomination which I served then was the only one to neglect such teaching, it would be sad. But the tragic truth is it is not the only one. The churches that train people to confront the reality of demonic activity are the exception - not the rule.

Is there a biblical commission which says Christians are to engage the enemy in spiritual warfare? I have come to see John 14:12-14 in the form of a commissioning of believers for spiritual warfare.

> Verily, verily, I say unto you, he that believeth on me, the works I do shall he do also; and greater works than these shall he do; because I go unto my Father. And whatsoever ye shall ask in my name, that will I do, that the Father may be glorified in the Son. If ye shall ask any thing in my name, I will do it.

In this commissioning there is no limiting time frame which says only the early Church was so commissioned. There is, also, no evidence here that only priests or other specially chosen leaders should continue His works. Nor is there anything in our Lord's words which would indicate it is optional, allowing believers to pick and choose what they will or will not do. To the contrary, it is clear all believers are to do all of Christ's work on earth until He comes.

In this light, it is time that the Church stop fostering a false peace and become the Church-militant. The lord confirms this in His own words:

> Think not that I am come to send peace on earth: I came not to send peace, but a sword. For I am come to set a man at variance against his father, and the daughter against her mother, and the daughter in law against her mother in law. And a man's foes shall be they of his own household. [Matt.10:34-36]

Our Lord knew full well how Satan excites the 'sin principle' fostering discontent within the family setting. He uses that same tactic to bring disharmony into the household of God. Therefore, it was necessary for our Lord to send a sword against the evil works of Satan. It is time for discerning among God's people so that the work of unclean spirits be recognized and warred against.

It is time for war! It is time for the Church to rise up and engage the enemy once again as was done by the Lord Jesus Christ. The offensive launched by Him against the bondages of Satan has been lost in modern Christianity. It is recognized, of course, that man brings many bondages

89

upon himself through ignorance. But it must also be acknowledged that the enemy lies in wait to exploit that ignorance. The Church must teach the reality of spiritual warfare because the lack of knowledge opens the door for destruction by the enemy. God Himself says, "My people are destroyed for lack of knowledge..." [Hosea 4:6] The Church must take responsibility in order that God's people not be destroyed through bondages allowed by ignorance.

It is with a sense of urgency that I write this final part of A TIME FOR WAR. Here you will find that unclean spirits still exist today and that Christians can indeed have demons and that they can be set free - gloriously free. Since it is God's plan to use believers to set men free, you will be shown the source and scope of the believer's authority. In this final part we will go through the common aspects of a deliverance/inner-healing session. Types of demonic activity will be described and the symptoms explained so that you will not be overcome or deceived through ignorance. The particular vocabulary of this ministry will be thoroughly defined.

It is my intention that the men and women of God be equipped to do battle. It is past time to rise up and do battle with our adversary, that old serpent, the devil. It is time to stop fighting over minor points of doctrine and unite in defeating the destroyer of men's souls. Let's put on the armor, lift up the shield of faith, take up the sword of the Spirit and go to battle. IT IS TIME FOR WAR!

CHAPTER 5

YOU CAN BE FREE!

The Christian and Demons

A persistent question among Christians concerns the possibility of believers being invaded by demonic forces. Among those who believe that a Christian cannot have a demon the argument usually follows one of two lines: the Holy Spirit will not (or cannot) inhabit the same body with an unclean spirit; or the Christian has been sealed by the Holy Spirit which prevents unclean spirits from invading the life of a believer.

Taking the last argument first we find the scriptural references to the sealing by the Holy Spirit in Eph. 1:13 and 4:30. This sealing is not in the sense of sealing a jar of fruit against contamination or even to preserve the purity of its contents. Rather, it refers to a mark or sign of ownership such as on a document. Such sealing is a sign to a believer that he/she is a child of God, the promised inheritance truly exists and that it will be obtained. (Many Bible translations speak of "demon possession." Such a translation tends to lend itself to the idea of ownership when actually, the original language of the New Testament seems to signify that a person is occupied or invaded, not owned, by demons. This is the apparent emphasis Jesus made in Mt. 12:43-45. Perhaps a better term is "demonized" rather than demon possessed.)

The other argument has two points and both must be true for the argument to hold up. First, every believer has the Holy Spirit and secondly, the Holy Spirit will not co-habitate in any way with a demon. The first point has been argued for centuries by sincere Christians and I doubt that I can successfully resolve the issue. Let it suffice that I believe conversion does not happen without the work of the Holy Spirit within a person bringing him/her to repentance and faith.

That brings us to the second point. If the Holy Spirit is required to effect the "new birth," it would be impossible for any demon-inhabited person to be converted if the point is true concerning the Holy Spirit's refusal to co-habitate with demons. The problem becomes more severe when it is realized the source of the argument is the proposition that the holy cannot abide contact with the evil. Consideration of this matter must take into account our human natures. If there is a person on the face of the earth who possesses a pure human nature free of satanic influence then the proposition will stand. But only one man passed that test - Jesus

Christ! If the Holy Spirit cannot dwell in the same body as demons, how could He possibly come into a living relationship with us while we are still in our corrupt human natures? An honest appraisal of any person's human nature, whether Christian or not, will reveal its intimate relationship with evil. The unredeemed human nature, according to the scriptures, is totally corrupt (Ps. 51:5; Rom. 7:18) and thus fully responsive to satanic influences. Nevertheless, at conversion the Holy Spirit comes into such a person bringing light and life.

The majority of persons we work with are professed Christians - people who know Jesus Christ as their personal Savior. They come because they are unable to fully submit to the lordship of Jesus Christ and enter into true sonship. They come because of depression, despair and other manifestations which are not of God but are identified in scripture as coming from Satan. It is not our policy to seek out demon harassed Christians; rather, it is they who come to us seeking to be freed from the hinderance of evil spirits in their lives.

God has provided ample resources to enable Christians to be free from demonic invasion but the effectiveness of such resources is limited to their being understood and used by believers. For example, the Bible says that if we resist the devil, he will flee from us (James 4:7.) What happens if the Christian, either through ignorance or deliberate neglect, does not resist? Is it reasonable for that person to expect God's protection to be in effect in his life? We are told in Ephesians 4:22 to "put off the old man." We are not told the Holy Spirit will do it for us. The scriptures also say to put on the full armor of God that we might withstand the wiles of the devil (Eph.6). Should a Christian neglect this admonition, the spiritual protection cannot be expected.

Satan is not allowed to do all that he may desire but he and his demons are permitted to function in many areas. All Christians are subject to temptation just as are all human beings. Satan knows his limitations and he also knows his rights and will exploit them to the fullest. If we are to take comfort in knowing God's protection through the presence of the Holy Spirit in our lives, it is imperative that we allow the Holy Spirit to direct all aspects of our lives. Whatever part of our life is not directed by the Holy Spirit is open to the control of another spirit. (This does not mean, however, the believer is simply a puppet.) Christians must become aware of what forces are working in their lives.

Evidence From Scripture

In the Old Testament we discover that the sin principle in men had manifested itself until God deemed it necessary to destroy man from the earth (Gen. 6:5.) Even after the flood, God declared the heart of man to be evil continually from his youth (Gen. 8:21.) The repeated falling into idolatry by God's chosen people is another indication of the human nature corrupted by the sin principle and responsive to the enticements of Satan (Ezk.23:30.) The sin principle is thoroughly responsive to the influence of the satanic kingdom and this provides the intimations of Satan's activity throughout the Old Testament record.

There is a clear statement in scripture that Satan blinds the minds of men, especially those who do not believe.

> In whom the god of this world hath blinded the minds of them which believe not, lest the light of the glorious gospel of Christ, who is the image of God, should shine unto them. [2 Cor 4:4]

But what about those who do believe? Paul is obviously speaking to believers when he writes:

> For though we walk in the flesh, we do not war after the flesh: ... Casting down imaginations, and every high thing that exalteth itself against the knowledge of God, and bringing into captivity every thought to the obedience of Christ; [2 Cor. 10:3,5]

> But I fear, lest by any means, as the serpent beguiled Eve trough his subtilty, so your minds should be corrupted from the simplicity that is in Christ. [2 Cor. 11:3]

These statements clearly show that Christians can and do walk in the flesh and strongly intimate that the mind of a Christian is thus subject to attack by Satan. Furthermore, in the very next verse (2 Cor 11:4) He warns about the possibility of receiving "another spirit which ye have not received,..." It would appear Paul believed it possible for Christians to come under attack, be deceived by Satan and his demons, and actually receive a spirit different from the Holy Spirit.

> But if ye have bitter envying and strife in your hearts, ...This wisdom descendeth not from above, but is earthly, sensual, devilish. For where envying and strife

is, there is confusion and every evil work. [James 3:14-16]

James, apparently, believed that Christians could have bitterness, envying, strife, confusion and evil works. This scripture clearly states such things are not from God or His kingdom but are of the earth, our carnal natures or the devil. James indicates that the sin principle working in Christians opens them up to demon activity. Finally, Paul warns concerning our times:

Now the Spirit speaketh expressly, that in the latter times some shall depart from the faith, giving heed to seducing spirits, and doctrines of devils; [1 Tim. 4:1]

It is quite apparent Paul foresaw it was not only possible, but likely, the devil was going to be able to seduce Christians to the point some would depart from the faith they had in Christ. The focus of scripture is that Christians can be invaded by demons.

Neither give place to the devil. ... Let him that stole steal no more: ... Let no corrupt communication proceed out of your mouth, ... And grieve not the Holy Spirit of God,... Let all bitterness, and wrath, and anger, and clamour, and evil speaking, be put away from you, with all malice: [Eph. 4:27-31]

The KJV uses the phrase "Neither give place to the devil" which some have taken to mean we should not move over when evil threatens. The NIV says "Do not give the devil a foothold" which gives the idea of not allowing Satan to find anything in our lives on which to start his evil work. The import of this scripture demonstrates it is possible for Satan to gain access to a Christian's life. The "foothold(s)" for Satan are listed: bitterness, wrath, etc. Unforgiveness is a wide-open entrance for Satan to gain access to a Christian's life. Paul says it gives Satan the advantage over us.

To whom ye forgive any thing, I forgive also: for if I forgave any thing, to whom I forgave it, for your sakes forgave I it in the person of Christ; Lest Satan should get an advantage of us: for we are not ignorant of his devices. [2 Cor. 2:10,11]

Jesus said we must forgive in order to obtain forgiveness and that if we have "aught against any" we must forgive [Mk.11:25.) It is

94

impossible to overemphasize the importance of forgiveness. Constantly, almost daily, we minister to Christians who have held unforgiveness for real or imagined wounds and have given Satan the opportunity to wreak havoc in their lives.

In his second letter to the Corinthians, Paul writes about what may be the most puzzling aspect of his life.

> And lest I should be exalted above measure through the abundance of revelations, there was given to me a thorn in the flesh, the messenger of Satan to buffet me, lest I should be exalted above measure. [2 Cor. 12:7]

Throughout history scholars and others have tried to figure out what it was that afflicted Paul. I am not going to attempt to diagnose the affliction but, rather, point out its source. Paul said it was a "messenger of Satan." The word here translated "messenger" is usually translated as "angel." Whether we like it or not, whether it fits our theology or not, the scripture is clear that "angels of Satan" are demons. There are other passages which speak of demon activity but let the conclusion of this matter rest in these words:

> Be sober, be vigilant; because your adversary the devil, as a roaring lion, walketh about, seeking whom he may devour: [1 Peter 5:8]

Surely Peter had no need to warn Christians about an enemy who could devour them if such were not possible. There is always the danger of falling into a carnal, false security which says "I am a believer; I am washed totally clean. Satan may approach but when I command him to leave, he flees." The experience of counseling hundreds of Christians proves to me that believers can be invaded by unclean spirits. (In addition, a person may be born with an unclean spirit inherited from parents or ancestors. See the section on "Sins of the Fathers.")

Invincibility to demonic invasion rests in submission to the Lord Jesus Christ and walking with the Holy Spirit in the process of sanctification. To be totally closed to demonic invasions, the believer must be totally led by the Holy Spirit in every decision and action. So it is that Peter warns Christians to be sober and vigilant lest Satan "devour" them.

Sin and Man

The basic doctrine of the Bible is the Love of God. This doctrine is not appreciated without the doctrine of Original Sin being understood. The Doctrine of Original sin teaches that with the fall of Adam and Eve into sin, all persons have since been conceived in sin. Sin, or evil is, therefore, an inherent part of all who are born on the earth. If it were not for the grace of God, manifested in the death and resurrection of Jesus Christ, all mankind would be doomed to eternal damnation.

I recognize that some teach there is a spark of goodness in each person but I still affirm that no child is born with such a spark. If all are not born with the sin principle (or original sin) then there is no need for Jesus' death and resurrection. Scripture states that all are born enemies of God, redeemed only through the shed blood of Jesus Christ (Rom. 8:7; John 14;6.) To clarify the issue, look at the following references:

> And God said, Let us make man in our image, after our likeness: ... So God created man in his own image, in the image of God created he him; male and female created he them. [Gen. 1:26,27]

The image of God consists of holiness and perfection and man was created with that image - perfect, without sin. However, man lost that image when Adam and Eve fell.

> And Adam lived an hundred and thirty years, and begat a son in his own likeness, after his image; ... [Gen. 5:3]

It is quite apparent that Adam did not conceive children after God's image of holiness but, rather, after his own fallen, sinful, corrupted nature. Since that time, all children are conceived in the image of corruption and sin.

> Behold, I was shapen in iniquity; and in sin did my mother conceive me. [Psalm 51:5]

This is not saying that sexual intercourse is sinful anymore than communication is corrupt even though we are warned about "corrupt communication" in the scriptures (Eph. 4:29.) This passage is simply saying that men and women produce others like themselves - corrupt children are the products of corrupt parents. This is the consequence of original sin - none escape it!

The effect of original sin is felt in all areas of man's life. The unregenerate person, whether he knows it or not, experiences the sin principle functioning in his spirit, soul and body. All are subject to its corruptive work. The psalmist, led by the Holy Spirit, spoke these words:

> The Lord looked down from heaven upon the children of men, to see if there were any that did understand, and seek God. They are all gone aside, they are all together become filthy, there is none that doeth good, no, not one. [Psalm 14:2,3]

The doctrine of original sin is difficult to comprehend unless it is also believed man is body, soul and spirit in nature. My own theological training leaned toward duality - body and soul only. However, this caused me a great deal of difficulty when I sought to understand the Apostle John's first epistle.

> If we say that we have not sinned, we make him a liar, and his word is not in us. [1:10]...

> If any man love the world, the love of the Father is not in him. For all that is in the world, the lust of the flesh, and the lust of the eyes, and the pride of life, is not of the Father, but is of the world. [2:15,16]

> Whosoever abideth in him sinneth not: whosoever sinneth hath not seen him, neither known him.[3:6]

John makes it rather clear that those who sin do not really know God or have his Word indwelling them. He strengthens his presentation with the following:

> Whosoever is born of God doth not commit sin; for his seed remaineth in him: and he cannot sin, because he is born of God. In this the children of God are manifest, and the children of the devil: whosoever doeth not righteousness is not of God, neither he that loveth not his brother.[3:9,10]

John was not speaking to unregenerate people. He was speaking to believers (see vs. 2:1.)

It would appear that John is in direct contradiction or else there is some way in which man becomes unable to sin. On the one hand, he says that all men sin and any person who denies his sinning is a liar. Moreover, that same person makes God out to be a liar and does not have God indwelling him. On the other hand, John says that those who are born of God not only do not sin, they are not even capable of sinning. I have observed a vast number of Christians and I find none that are free of sin. (I have also met some who believe they do not sin, however, their lives betray them.)

I have come to understand that John is saying that there is a part of man which is incapable of sinning after conversion, while another part retains the ability to sin and actually seeks to sin. Now if man is only body and soul, then his body sins and his soul is pure. But this runs contrary to our Lord's words.

> But those things which proceed out of the mouth come forth from the heart; and they defile the man. For out of the heart proceed evil thoughts, murders, adulteries, fornications, thefts, false witness, blasphemies: These are the things which defile a man: [Matt. 15:18-20] A good man out of the good treasure of his heart bringeth forth that which is good; and an evil man out of the evil treasure of his heart bringeth forth that which is evil: for of the abundance of the heart his mouth speaketh. [Luke 6:45]

It is rather evident from these passages that if a man sins, it is from the heart; but John wrote that if a man sins he is not of God; yet we know believers sin after conversion and to deny this makes God a liar. This contradiction is resolved if it is agreed that there is some part of man that does not sin after conversion. That part of man is not the body (which commits sin) nor the soul (from which sin originates.)

It is in the book of Hebrews that the part of man that does not sin is revealed.

> For the word of God is quick, and powerful, and sharper than any two-edged sword, piercing even to the dividing asunder of soul and spirit, and of the joints and marrow, and is a discerner of the thoughts and intents of the heart. [Heb.4:12]

Without going into a detailed exegesis of this passage, it is evident that there is a difference between the soul and spirit of man and that the make-up of man is body, soul and spirit. This seems to agree with

God's promise in Ezekiel:

> A new heart also will I give you, and a new spirit will I
> put within you: and I will take away the stony heart out
> of your flesh, and I will give you an heart of flesh.
> [Ezk.36:26]

You will note that here the spirit and heart (or soul) are separated
as they were in the Hebrews passage. Some may say that the Ezekiel
statement is merely a hebraism (a Hebrew literary device) used to
emphasize a point. However, it seems to go beyond this as it agrees so
clearly with the Hebrews passage. While it is true that scripture sometimes speaks of soul and spirit synonymously, it also speaks of each
singularly at other times.

In the light of the scriptural evidence, I have come to see that if
man is spirit, soul and body, it is possible that some part of the believer
cannot sin. That part which is unable to sin is the believer's spirit. Titus
3:5 speaks to this matter:

> ... according to his mercy he saved us, by the washing of
> regeneration, and renewing of the Holy Ghost; [Titus
> 3:5]

We also read in Peter's first epistle concerning the sanctifying of
one's soul through the work of the Holy Spirit:

> Being born again, not of corruptible seed, but of incor-
> ruptible, by the word of God, which liveth and abideth
> for ever. [1 Peter 1:23]

Now, how shall we use what we have gained from God's word?
From Genesis we learned man was created in the image of God's holiness.
However, that image became corrupt in body, soul, and spirit because of
man's fall into sin. In the New Testament we learned that man's spirit can
be restored on earth. This is accomplished by God's Spirit working
through the word in which He promised to put a new spirit in us. He is
speaking of the Holy Spirit coming into man's spirit. When the Holy
Spirit enters the spirit of a person, that person's spirit is renewed or born
again. Titus called it the "renewing of the Holy Ghost."

The Apostle John wrote that when that happens to a man "he
cannot sin, because he is born of God." What is born of God - the man's
soul? No! Is it his body? No! It is the spirit that is born of God and cannot

remain the battleground between the forces of evil and the reborn spirit which is directed by the Holy Spirit!

How Demons Enter Christians

The most common opening in a Christian's life is the allowing of a foothold or giving place to the devil as we learned from Eph. 4:27. How does this happen? A foothold is given by the Christian through ignorance of truth, passivity, deception, harboring known sin, failure to forgive, undisciplined thinking, unbelief, doubt, lack of prayer, independence, pride, selfishness, anxiety, emotional excesses, lack of watchfulness, pliability, vacillation in faith and believing lies by wicked spirits. This is by no means an exhaustive listing. Rather, it is an attempt to show how obvious are the means whereby the believer gives place to Satan.

The strongest Christian is subject to giving a foothold to Satan. It is a common experience in this ministry to see a reaction of shock and dismay by a believer after a simple prayer taking back the ground from demons in areas that the person did not realize had been given over to unclean spirits. This reaction is not because of the prayer - it comes when demons manifest themselves and leave.

Any unforgiven hurt or slight by another may open the door to demonic invasion. A passive attitude towards living the Christian life often leaves the door open. Emotional excesses are closely monitored by Satan to attempt to hold a person in emotional bondage. Periods of deep sorrow are opportunities for a spirit of depression to work its way into the life of a Christian. Satan and his forces are ever alert to all openings.

It is important to remember that demonic forces cannot enter the spirit of a Christian, that is the dwelling place of the Holy Spirit. It is the soul which is invaded, involving the will, emotions, senses, etc. In the Christian, demonic forces may invade and occupy areas of the soul, but never the whole soul since that would mean complete ownership.

The following illustrations may serve to describe what happens to the unregenerate person and the converted person in whom the Holy Spirit dwells. In Figure No. 1, the spirit, soul and body are under Satanic bondage because the person does not know Jesus Christ as Savior and Lord. Satan will use a lustful circumstance to tempt the person. God allows the action to take place since Satan only functions within the limitations imposed by God. You may recall that Job said:

100

What I feared has come upon me; what I dreaded has happened to me. I have no peace, no quietness; I have no rest, but only turmoil. [Job 3:25,26 NIV]

Satan was allowed to test him as he opened himself up to Satanic attack.

In the illustration, a lustful situation has occurred and is being used, by Satan, to tempt the person. Now a decision must be made to resist or yield. Since this person is not a Christian, it is likely the decision will be made to yield and the result will be a sinful action. This pattern will be repeated several times until a habit is formed and then Satan may send in a demon of lust to control the actions of the person.

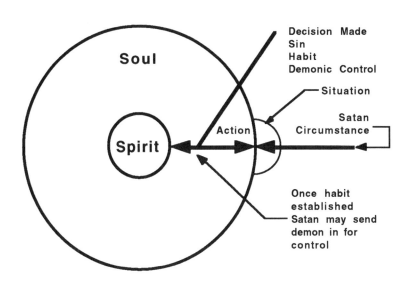

Figure 1.

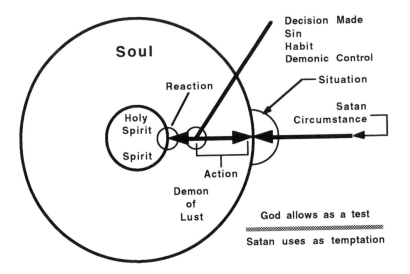

Figure 2.

Figure No. 2 pictures a Christian in whom the Holy Spirit dwells and whose spirit cannot sin as we learned in 1 John 3. However, because of the presence of an unclean spirit at birth or habits prior to becoming a Christian, this person has a demon of lust. When the temptation is presented, a battle in the soul ensues. This person's spirit, under the leadership of the Holy Spirit, resists the temptation while the unclean spirit attempts to control the soul and force a decision to yield. In addition, the body's natural desire is aroused and makes its own demands. The battle is often fierce and the person is in great turmoil.

Should the person successfully resist the temptation, he or she will experience the joy of victory but find it terribly short-termed. The demon will not rest and will continue to take advantage of every possible lustful situation. If the person yields, then guilt will be added and used by Satan to harass and torment. Such a person will often despair and come to believe that the Holy Spirit has left and the person will no longer consider him/herself to be a Christian. Satan has then won a terrible victory.

A devout, sincere believer, though not invaded by a demon from the past life, may still fall victim to Satan's wiles. The carnal nature is still functioning in the soul and body of a believer. When a believer yields to the desires of the old nature that is "giving place to the devil" and if enough place is given a foothold may be established. It then becomes necessary to expel the demonic force in the authority of Jesus' name and the sooner the better.

I have used lust as the example but what I have said about lust is equally true for all the activities of the enemy. Rejection, fear, bitterness, hatred, infirmity and a host of other bondages are all weapons Satan uses in the hope of destroying believers and, eventually, all mankind. Satan will not succeed but that does not diminish the battle nor give him pause in his efforts.

The believer need not lose heart because the enemy is able to exploit the carnal aspects of our humanity. Jesus came to set the captives free. His life and ministry demonstrated absolute authority over the powers of darkness. The crucifixion and resurrection brought complete triumph over the satanic principalities (Col. 2:14,15.) Then when Jesus ascended on high He sent the gift of the Holy Spirit validating the transference of authority to every believer (Mark 16:15-18; Acts 1:8.)

Fellow believer, you may now be convinced that Satan has gained footholds in your life but do not despair. You have great and powerful resources available to set you free and make you an overcomer. Submit yourself to the Lord, resist the devil and he will flee from you because greater is He that is in you than he that is in the world. If you should be unsuccessful in your efforts to overcome the unclean spirits that have invaded your life, seek out other knowledgeable believers who will do battle for you. In the name of Jesus Christ they can cast out demons and break the bondages in your life.

The following sections of this book will reinforce the understanding of the believer's authority and methods of doing battle with unclean spirits. Read them and work them in your life and in the lives of other believers bound by Satan and his hosts. You can be free and you can set others free.

CHAPTER 6

AUTHORITY OF THE BELIEVER

There is a song sung in charismatic circles which says:
Majesty - Kingdom authority,
Flows from His throne - unto His own -
Whose anthem we raise.

What is the essence of "Kingdom authority?" And over whom is it exercised? I have seen some who claim kingdom authority and then exercise it over fellow believers with devastating results. I have also seen churches hold believers in various kinds of bondage as they used so-called kingdom authority. I am writing of a kingdom authority which serves to glorify the name of Jesus Christ and is exercised over the satanic kingdom for the release and blessing of God's people. That authority is given by the Lord Jesus Christ to every believer in order to meet all circumstance.

In John 14:12 our Lord commissions every believer to continue His ministry of love, power, and authority. Jesus exercised authority over Satan, the enemy of God, and broke his hold upon mankind. Scripture says Jesus came to destroy the works of the devil [1 John 3:8]. Christ's commission to every believer includes authority for the destruction of the works of Satan. The effective use of that authority comes only through those who know who they are in Christ. To come into confrontation with the satanic kingdom demands an understanding of one's relationship with the heavenly kingdom and especially its king, Jesus Christ!

To begin with, at conversion a person comes into a unique relationship with the Lord Jesus Christ. Paul says:

... we are buried with Him by baptism into death: that like as Christ was raised up from the dead by the glory of the Father, even so we also should walk in newness of life. [Rom. 6:4]

Whereas once the believer was able only to walk in the old corrupt nature, now, by the regenerating power of the Holy Spirit, he has the capability to walk in newness of life. A new nature has been born within. With that new birth comes an intimate union with the Lord Jesus Christ.

Even when we were dead in sins, [God] hath quickened us together with Christ ..... And made us to sit together in heavenly places in Christ Jesus. [Eph. 2:5-6]

According as his divine power hath given unto us all things that pertain unto life and godliness, through the knowledge of him that hath called us to glory and virtue: whereby are given unto us exceeding great and precious promises: that by these ye might be partakers of the divine nature, having escaped the corruption that is in the world through lust. [II Pet. 1:3-4]

For we are members of His body, His flesh, and of His bones." [Eph. 5:30]

From these passages one is enabled to see that through intimate union with the Lord Jesus Christ the believer becomes a member of Christ's body, His flesh and His bones. Likewise that person is a partaker of Christ's divine nature and sits with Him in heavenly places. That intimate union with the Lord Jesus Christ together with His commission in John 14:12 gives the believer full authority to continue Christ's ministry until He comes again in His glory.

One aspect of kingdom authority of which every believer must be aware concerns not only authority but also every blessing bestowed upon man. God speaking through the prophet Isaiah set forth a principle which extends into our own day.

But I had pity for mine holy name, which the house of Israel had profaned among the heathen, wither they went. Therefore say unto the house of Israel, Thus saith the Lord God; I do not this for your sakes, O house of Israel, but for mine holy name's sake, ... And I will sanctify my great name which was profaned among the heathen, ... when I shall be sanctified in you before their eyes. [Ezk. 36:21-23]

Though this was spoken to the nation of Israel it is also true for our day. God exercises kingdom authority through His children not for their sakes alone but for the sake of His holy name! The principle set forth in that day still holds true in our day: all works are done for the glory of His name! Kingdom authority is never to be abused or misused for to do so profanes the name of God and the name of the Lord Jesus Christ must never be profaned.

The exercise of Kingdom authority cannot be fully realized until the believer comes to grips with the desire of his own heart. Before the fall of Adam and Eve the desire of their hearts was directed toward God and His desire for them. Through the deceptive work of Satan and the introduction of the sin principle, their desire turned from God to the flesh. With the knowledge of good and evil came also the corruption of man's desire.

This truth is seen in God's words to Eve, ".... thy desire shall be to thy husband, and he shall rule over thee." [Gen.3:16] Before the fall the mind, intellect and emotional structure in Adam and Eve was God-oriented. Now, with the knowledge of good and evil, their minds, intellects and emotions became subject to a mixture of good and evil. Now the desire of their hearts was not always in harmony with God's desire for their lives. That remains true to our own day for we have the freedom of the will to choose between good and evil.

In Jesus we see the perfect example of human desire giving way to the desire of God. He said, ".... O my father, if it be possible, let this cup pass from me: nevertheless not as I will, but as Thou wilt." [Matt. 26:39] Jesus, according to His human nature, could be tempted by the temptations of the world. Scripture says He was true man and true God, therefore, according to His human nature, the desire of His heart could be drawn away from that of the Father. He chose to follow the desire of His Father and remained untainted by sin.

Those who walk and live as the Spirit leads turn the desire of their hearts to the ways of the Heavenly Father. Every true believer has the power to overrule the evil desires which arise in the mind and intellect. When the believer chooses to allow his human spirit, filled with the Holy Spirit, to direct his or her life that person is then in the process of bringing the desire of the heart into harmony with the Father's desire. With that harmony the person is fully enabled and empowered to exercise the authority of the Name of Jesus Christ and the power of His blood. It is only as the desire of the heart is turned from the world and back to God that the believer can truly exercise God-given authority over the power of the enemy.

Scripture speaks of the authority conferred upon those who believe:

He that believeth and is baptized shall be saved: but he that believeth not shall be damned. And these signs shall follow them that believe: in My name shall they cast out devils; they shall speak with new tongues; they shall take up serpents; and if they drink any deadly thing, it shall not hurt them; they shall lay hands on the sick, and they shall recover. [Mark 16:16-18]

There are those who question the validity of this passage, saying that it is not found in some of the early Greek manuscripts. I have no intention of attempting to argue the matter. However, if the passage is accepted as coming from divine inspiration then some profound things must be considered.

The passage states that certain signs are to be evident in the lives of those who believe:

1. In the name of Jesus Christ they shall cast out devils. (Nothing is indicated here that this is optional for the believer. It says they shall do it!)

2. Believers shall speak with new tongues. (Regardless of how one interprets this, a new form of communication will be evident in the life of the believer!)

3. Deadly things shall not harm them!

4. They shall lay hands upon the sick and the sick shall recover!

This is a brief and concise outline of the authority which is given to every believer.

Since there may be some people who have difficulty accepting this passage, let's consider other passages which are unquestioned. Jesus gave authority to His disciples and we know they exercised that authority.

Then He called His twelve disciples together, and gave them power and authority over all devils, and to cure diseases. [Lk. 9:1]

And they departed, and went preaching through the towns, and healing everywhere. [Lk. 9:6]

Later we read of this same authority being given to seventy disciples:

Behold, I give unto you the power to tread on serpents and scorpions, and over all the power of the enemy: and nothing shall by any means hurt you. Notwithstanding in this rejoice not, that the spirits are subject unto you; but rather rejoice, because your names are written in heaven. [Lk 10:19,20]

The last portion of this passage is included because it contains a valuable lesson. First, it speaks clearly of the believer's authority. Secondly, it reminds us of spiritual priorities. It is more important for our names to be written in the Lamb's Book of Life than for spirits to be subject to our authority. However, this does not diminish the truth that believers have authority over unclean spirits and this authority is to be a part of the ongoing ministry of every believer.

Peter exercised the authority given to him to bring healing to a lame man (Acts 3:6.) That same authority was evident when Tabitha was raised from the dead (Acts 9:36.) Again, that authority was clearly evident in the healing of a man afflicted with palsy (Acts 9:32.)

Paul also exercised authority when he commanded a spirit of divination out of a woman in Philippi (Acts 16:16.) Special miracles were done by Paul:

And God wrought special miracles by the hands of Paul: so that from his body were brought unto the sick hand-kerchiefs or aprons, and the diseases departed from them, and the evil spirits went out of them. [Acts 19:11,12]

The words recorded in the 16th chapter of Mark concerning serpents and believers was confirmed in the life of Paul:

And when Paul had gathered a bundle of sticks, and laid them on the fire, there came a viper out of the heat, and fastened on his hand..... And he shook off the beast into the fire, and felt no harm. . . . after they looked a great while and saw no harm come to him they changed their minds, and said that he was a god. [Acts 28:3]

108

The fulfillment of Mark 16 was not limited to the Twelve or other apostles. Converts, from the beginning, went out preaching the Gospel and performing signs and wonders. Sometimes at the cost of their lives.

> And Stephen, full of faith and power, did great wonders and miracles among the people. [Acts 6:8]....they were cut to the heart, and they gnashed on him with their teeth. ....then they cried out with a loud voice .... and ran upon him with one accord, and cast him out of the city, and stoned him: .... [Acts 7:54-58]

> .... the people with one accord gave heed unto those things which Philip spoke, hearing and seeing the miracles which he did. For unclean spirits, crying with a loud voice, came out of many that were possessed with them: and many taken with palsies, and that were lame, were healed. [Acts 8:6,7]

> Then Simon himself believed also and when he was baptized, he continued with Philip, and wondered, beholding the miracles and signs which were done." [Acts 8:13]

> And there was a certain disciple at Damascus, named Ananias: .... And the Lord said unto him, Arise, and go into the street which is called Straight, and enquire ... for one called Saul, of Tarsus: for, behold, he prayeth, ... And Ananias went his way, and entered into the house; and putting his hands on him said, Brother Saul, the Lord, even Jesus, that appeared unto thee in the way as thou camest, hath sent me, that thou mightest receive they sight, and be filled with the Holy Ghost. And immediately there fell from his eyes as it had been scales: and he received sight forthwith, and arose, and was baptized. [Acts 9:10-18]

Many Christians will acknowledge that one may pray for healings and expect the same to happen. They will also acknowledge that the Apostles exercised authority and power over illness, disease and even unclean spirits. But, as they survey Christendom today, doubt and unbelief enter in, especially concerning individual authority. They reason that God may anoint certain persons with authority and power for special healing ministries, but for the individual Christian to entertain any thoughts of exercising such authority is beyond comprehension.

However, the words of our Lord seem to clearly refute such thinking:

> Believe Me that I am in the Father, and the Father in Me:
> or else believe Me for the very work's sake. Verily,
> verily, I say unto you. He that believeth on Me, the works
> that I do shall he do also; and greater works than these
> shall he do; because I go unto My Father. .... If ye shall ask
> anything in My name, I will do it. .... And I will pray the
> Father, and He shall give you another Comforter, that
> He may abide with you forever, even the Spirit of Truth;
> whom the world cannot receive, because it seeth Him
> not, neither knoweth Him: but ye know Him; for He
> dwelleth with you, and shall be in you. .... But the
> Comforter, which is the Holy Ghost, whom the Father
> will send in My name, He shall teach you all things and
> bring all things to your remembrance, whatsoever I have
> said unto you. [John 14:11-26]

In the first years of my ministry I was not able to preach or teach from this passage. I could not do the works which Jesus did in His ministry nor was I witnessing anyone else doing them. There were a few radio and television personalities who claimed to be exercising such authority and power, but there was little, if any, evidence of the works which Jesus Christ did occurring in the church on earth. To even question why the works were not in evidence generally brought the response that one must always qualify such prayers with, "If it be Thy will ...."

I saw the need for healings among the church people I served and I prayed that God might heal them out of His mercy and compassion. I truly believed it was not His will that they should suffer. Likewise, I prayed that He would somehow deliver others from their strange and heavy bondages. Again, I was sure it could not be His will that they continue to carry such burdens.

When I spoke about this to fellow pastors and others in positions of church authority, I heard that God honors the sufferings of His people. Therefore, if they were suffering, it was God's will and they should suffer in dignity in order that the Father might be glorified. To pray that the person be healed or delivered would be in direct contradiction to the will of God.

I was constantly confronted with the Lord's words in John 14 and yet I could not do them! It became imperative I examine the works of Jesus which I, as a believer, was to do. I found Luke 4:18 outlines the work

Jesus was to do and the Gospels record clearly the works He did. So it became apparent, at least to me, John 14:12 was not an optional matter but a statement of fact and a commission to the entire body of Christ.

Our Lord expects us to believe the words spoken to the disciples:

> .... I say unto you, If ye have faith as a grain of mustard seed, ye shall say unto this mountain, Remove hence to yonder place and it shall remove; and nothing shall be impossible unto you. [Matt. 17:20]

The mountain facing the disciples that day was a dumb and deaf spirit. The mountains facing believers today include not only dumb and deaf spirits but other spirits, afflictions, diseases and every work of the enemy. The authority and power to do the works which Jesus did are no less available for the believer of today than for the disciples of Jesus's day. Praise God!

The difficulty does not lie in the continuity of kingdom authority; rather the problem is with Christians believing, appropriating and exercising this power. Jesus Christ is the same "yesterday, today and forever" and His promises have not been withdrawn. "The gifts and callings of God are without repentance." (Rom. 11:29) They are for the Church of this present day. As we continue studying, keep in mind that kingdom authority is to be conferred on every believer. While individual believers differ in the particular ministry to which each is called, none are without the provision of God to fully engage the enemy and emerge victorious.

Having examined our authority as believers to engage in spiritual warfare, let us next examine the weapons of such warfare. Paul declares:

> For the weapons of our warfare are not carnal, but mighty through God to the pulling down of strong holds; [2 Cor.10:4]

This effectively places our battling on a plane strange to the natural man. We cannot overcome Satan by physical strength, natural intellect or the usual weapons of war. These battles will be fought in spiritual realms and with spiritual weapons. But we need not fear for these weapons are "mighty" (i.e. effective.)

111

CHAPTER 7

KNOWING THE ENEMY

Symptoms of Demonic Activity

A young minister called me one day seeking information concerning demonic activity and its symptoms. He was concerned about one of his members who he thought might be experiencing demonic attacks. He had led the woman to an acceptance of the Lord Jesus Christ as her personal savior. The first indication of trouble had come about two months later when she shared with him that voices, speaking from within, were threatening to kill her. She also related that during worship services they would tell her to rip off all her clothing and to strike various members of the congregation.

At a Sunday evening service, in desperation, she asked the pastor and congregation for prayer to free her from the tormenting voices. As they began the woman cried out that she was being bitten by demons. To the amazement of those present, bright red blotches appeared on her face and arms. Soon other parts of her body were covered with what looked like bites. She screamed that the demons were burning her with power-rays and she slumped to the floor in a faint. After much prayer she regained consciousness and was taken home. The attacks continued in her home and especially during worship services.

The young minister asked if we thought the problem might actually be demonic. He was positive she had received the Lord's salvation and had been cleansed of all evil. He was also convinced a Christian could not possibly have an unclean spirit since an unclean spirit cannot be in the same body in which the Holy Spirit dwells. After much discussion by phone he asked to bring her to us for counseling. Before the session closed demonic activity exploded within the woman and she became violent. There was no doubt left in his mind that she was indwelt by unclean spirits. It would take many more sessions to see her set free.

Such a scenario would leave little doubt with any sincere observer and is the type many believe to be the usual manifestation of demonic invasion. However, there are symptoms more subtle than these which are frequently passed off as idiosyncracies or character traits when in reality they are demonic. The dictionary definition of idiosyncracy is:

1. Any tendency, characteristic, mode of expression, or

the like, peculiar to an individual. 2. The physical constitution peculiar to an individual. 3. A peculiarity of the physical or the mental constitution esp. susceptibility toward drugs, food, etc. [American College Dictionary, 1960, Random House, Inc.. page 599.]

A woman came for counsel because of frequent attacks of depression. She lived in a facility for elderly people able to care for themselves. She was in her late sixties or early seventies and had come to know Jesus Christ in a personal way in her teen years. She said she was "Spirit-filled." She had never married though the desire for marriage had been very strong in her life. Most of her adult life was marked with periods of depression ranging from moderate to severe in intensity. Now in the closing years of her life the periods of depression were increasing in occurrence and intensity with no apparent physical or psychological reason.

During the first session I found my mind returning again and again to the word "rape". As I observed this beautiful, grand-motherly woman I could not understand why that word kept coming into my mind. I cautiously inquired if there had been an incident of rape within her immediate family. She responded quickly, "Oh my yes! I was raped when I was in my early teens."

She tearfully shared the guilt and shame which had so bound her that she could tell no one what had happened. I was the first person to ever know. She had not told her parents because of guilt nor her pastor for fear of coming under condemnation. Because of the guilt and shame she had turned away every man who gave any indication of a desire to marry her. Thus it was she never married, never bore children, nor knew the joy of grand-children.

A number of people had counseled her that she need only think on positive things to get the personality trait or idiosyncracy under control. What sincere people had failed to see was that the idiosyncracy was actually the symptomatic evidence of a deeper bondage. The root cause of the depression was demonic in nature. When authority was exercised over the strong men of rape, guilt, shame and depression, forcing them to depart from her, all symptoms of depression ceased. To my knowledge they have never returned.

A young woman came seeking ministry because of frequent episodes of depression which began in her early teen years. She also sought healing for asthmatic attacks which ranged from mild to debili-

113

tating. Doctors had been unable to determine an organic cause for the attacks. During the course of ministry the Holy Spirit caused the woman to remember being forced into oral sex by her grandfather at age three. At that point of the session the strongman of incest was commanded out. Then the Holy Spirit revealed a demonic stronghold of asthmatic infirmity which was also commanded out. It became clear to me that the trauma of the strangling and gagging accompanying the oral sex was the root cause of the asthmatic attacks.

The young woman reported a week later that all symptoms of depression and asthma were gone. There have been no reports of the return of either. I could understand the depression involved but I would never have associated incest with asthma. It took the work of the Holy Spirit to reveal the connection and bring real healing.

We know from scripture that the Lord does not give Christians a spirit of fear (2 Tim. 1:7.) Yet there are many who suffer from unexplainable fears in their lives. With the Holy Spirit's leading, many of these fears are traced back to traumatic events in early infancy and childhood which opened the door for unclean spirits to enter. One such case involved a woman in her mid-twenties who experienced feelings of uneasiness whenever she was with her mother. The relationship with her mother had been good as far back as she could recall yet she often felt fear and undertones of anger. The Holy Spirit was asked to probe her subconscious mind to determine the cause.

As we waited, the young woman began to exhibit signs of anxiety and uneasiness. She said, "I do not understand what I am feeling but I feel like I am completely enveloped in something and I see only darkness all about me." At that point I sensed the Holy Spirit had caused her to remember when she was in her mother's womb. Suddenly she screamed, "Oh no! She's going to kill me with that knife." I immediately commanded the strongmen of murder and abortion out of her. Then the demons of fear and anger were also commanded out. No longer does she have feelings of fear and anger in the presence of her mother. The symptoms were subtle and the true cause deeply hidden in the subconscious mind. Only the insight of the Holy Spirit led to her healing.

Some traumatic events border on the bizarre but some are rather common, such as locking a child in a dark closet for punishment. Another rather common cause is the use of scare stories to frighten a child into obedience. As the years pass by the unclean spirits use every opportunity to exploit common incidents to bring that fear to the surface. Counsel to exercise greater faith may bring some relief but complete healing usually comes when the spirits causing the fear are cast out.

Case after case could be cited where personality traits could easily be attributed to the old nature and frequently that is the counsel given. On many occasions Christian leaders have come to us crying out to be released from tormenting and driving sexual desires. Some had even considered leaving the ministry because the tormenting lusts made them feel they were hypocrites. In discussing these things with professional counselors and ministers I am often told that such problems are the products of unbridled carnal natures, the result of environmental influences or little more than personality quirks. (Perhaps the worst counsel is that such driven individuals just do not have enough faith.) However, when the possibility of demonic control is explored the Holy Spirit often brings light and freedom for the afflicted person.

Some Christians continually fight losing battles against depression, rage, envy and jealousy. I minister to some who repeatedly battle with thoughts of murder and suicide. A number of years in a pulpit and counseling ministry has led me to see that such torments are not simply idiosyncracies, character traits, or personality defects. Nor are they the result of a lack of faith on the part of the afflicted. More often than may be suspected, these are symptoms of deep rooted demonic strongholds.

Far too many of God's people are held in bondages by an enemy who robs them of the peace and joy which should be theirs as Christians. Those in ministry should be able to offer such people more than a word of sympathy or an exhortation to stronger faith. There must be a willingness to break out of theological shells and give prayerful consideration to the possibility that what is happening in the lives of fellow believers may be symptoms of demonic control. To ignore this possibility may mean sentencing a child of God to continual bondage.

A tell-tale sign of demonic control manifests itself in compulsive behavior over which the believer has difficulty gaining control. An extreme example in scripture is the account of the Gaderene demoniac (Luke 8:26.) Scripture describes symptoms of demonic activity within a person when it describes tormenting spirits as foul, lying, unclean, evil and deceiving. When someone comes seeking help and confesses that he or she has little or no control over perverse thoughts or actions, continued stretching of the truth, outright lying, various compelling lusts of the flesh and mind, and other driving compulsive behavior, the possibility of demonic control must be considered.

Some common symptoms of demonic activity are despair, anxiety, depression, unworthiness, insecurity, fear (of all kinds,) craving, wrath, bitterness, unforgiveness, rebellion, jealousy and heaviness. These symptoms center in the areas of the mind and the will but the effect of them may be found in the body also. The body may manifest symptoms of infirmity, disease, malady, fatigue and even death. While it is true many of these symptoms may come from within the old nature, they also may be symptoms of something much more deeply rooted. In the area of compulsive behavior dare we, as servants of the Lord, overlook, for any reason, the possibility of demonic control. Jesus used many means to effect healings including casting out demons. We, His ministering servants, should do no less!

Someone may come for ministry because of a feeling of heaviness. The expression of the problem might be:

Life has become a real drag. There is no meaning to anything anymore. My friends try to help but I am sick and tired of sympathy and being told to "think positive." All I want to do is sit and cry. I have no interest in my family, job, church or anything else. I thought about killing myself but God wont allow that. Maybe He will be merciful and let me die.

These may come across as attitudes but in most cases by the Holy Spirit's leading the Christian counselor will be shown that the individual is being tormented by spirits of heaviness (suicide, despair, hopelessness, and even a death wish are often present.)

Another common concern voiced by those seeking ministry is an inability to freely communicate with God. Their religious life is above reproach; if the church doors are open they will be there; worship and praise is sought with gusto. Yet, there seems to be a void in their personal relationship with the Lord. Soon after the worship service the joy and good feelings begin to drain away and God seems to be aloof. The Word of God will also tend to be closed to the reader.

Here again, with the leading of the Holy Spirit, we have found the source of the problem is often one of spiritual whoredom where the form of religion has replaced true spiritual worship. The emotional side of worship and praise replaces the Spirit-directed relationship with the Lord or the charisma of a religious leader has become the point of contact with the Lord. (This can infect the whole body of believers.) When these things occur, spirits of spiritual whoredom and spiritual idolatry will frequently lure the believer away from a close personal relationship with the Lord.

It is not unusual to find a spirit which answers to the name of "smothering." Especially where there has been some traumatic event which involved a closing off of one's breath. I think of a woman who came for counsel because she was tormented with dream in which her breathing was being cut off. There were other times when she would experience smothering for no apparent reason. The source of the problem was revealed through the gift of discerning. The Holy Spirit took the woman to an incident when she was very young. She saw and experienced being taken to surgery for a tonsillectomy. When the mask in the hand of the anesthesiologist descended to her face, panic and fear immediately flooded in accompanied by smothering. Spirits of fear, panic and smothering had entered in during that incident and arose to torment her whenever a circumstance would trigger the memory.

It is essential that any person entering into the arena of spiritual warfare be able to recognize the symptoms of demonic activity. When a brother or sister comes confessing a fault or an affliction, the ministering person must discern the source of the problem. Is it rising from the old nature not yet brought into submission to the new (spiritual) nature which is directed by the Holy Spirit? If the problem is with the old nature scripture reminds us:

> ... whosoever is born of God overcometh the world: and this is the victory that overcometh the world, even our faith. [I John 5:4]

But where does the "overcoming of the world" take place? There may be some who because of their religious training are left with the idea, as I was, that overcoming the world takes place in city streets, mission fields and the hell spots of the world. Overcoming of the world takes place first and foremost within the individual.

First, the old nature within each of us must be brought into submission to our human spirit which is indwelt by the Holy Spirit. If the old nature is not under submission to the Spirit then the Word of God and Christian counseling is in order. Then, and only then, can there be a moving out into the world to confront the work of the enemy there.

> He that overcometh, the same shall be clothed in white raiment; and I will not blot his name out of the book of

life, but I will confess his name before My Father, and before His angels. [Rev. 3:5]

Spirit Of Passivity

Passivity is such a subtle trap of the enemy I feel it necessary to deal with it separately from the general symptoms of demonic activity. Many Christians are entrapped, to some degree, without realizing it. The manifestations are written off as idiosyncracies or infirmities. Passive Christians will be heard to say they would be more active in church things but they are over-strained, over-taxed, without the necessary gifting, too timid, nervous and so forth. Passivity is overlooked by many who are counseling. It should be given more attention.

The word passivity is not a term found in scripture. The words idleness and sluggard imply passivity is involved.

Go to the ant, thou sluggard; consider her ways and be wise.... provideth her meat in the summer, and gathereth her food in the harvest. ... (Proverbs 6:6)

I believe passivity can be defined as the sin of omission. It is the sin of not doing those things which the Lord expects of a believer. The American College Dictionary defines passive as:

1. not acting, or not attended with or manifested in open or positive action; passive resistance. 2. inactive, quiescent, or inert. 3. suffering action, acted upon, or being the object of action, (opposed to active). 4. receiving, or characterized by the reception of, impressions from without. 5. produced by or due to external agency. 6. suffering, receiving, or submitting without resistance.

The writers of the Epistles urged the followers of Christ away from passiveness into active and power filled lives. For instance, Romans 12 (also see Eph. 4:27):

.... present your bodies a living sacrifice, holy, acceptable unto God, which is your reasonable service. And be not conformed to this world: but be ye transformed by the renewing of your mind, that ye may prove what is that good, and acceptable, and perfect, will of God. [vs. 1,2]

Not slothful in business; ... [vs. 11]

Distributing to the necessity of saints; ... [vs. 13]

The believer is to take positive steps toward changing the way of life in order to come into harmony with the will of God. There is no indication that the believer is to lay back and wait for the mind to be renewed. There is to be active control over the body, not a passive waiting, to bring it into position as a living sacrifice. Renewing is to be actively sought after as spiritual service to the Lord.

Scripture does not indicate that the believer is to be inactive or passive in his walk.

But ye have not so learned Christ; if so be that ye have heard him, and have been taught of him, as the truth is in Jesus: that ye put off concerning the former conversation the old man, which is corrupt according to the deceitful lusts; and be renewed in the spirit of your mind: and that ye put on the new man, which after God is created in righteousness and true holiness. [Eph. 4:20-24]

The new man is a creation of God, but the believer must put it on. That is to say, he cannot passively await the action of the new man to manifest itself. To the contrary, there must be the exercise of the will to put off the old and to take on the new which is created by God. The believer must exercise the human will in harmony with the will of the Father.

Passivity in the life of a believer is a loss of self-control. A principle of creation is the freedom and ability to exercise one's own will in harmony with the will of God. Whenever that freedom is forfeited that person moves into a state of passivity. Rather than being the initiator of action, the person becomes the object acted upon. The powers of darkness desire that the life of the believer should be a passive object acted upon.

It is the desire of the evil kingdom that the believer remain inactive or passive to the new creation - the new man. There is a song which speaks about "surrendering all to Jesus". It is an admirable thought but if misunderstood it can open legal ground to the enemy. God does not take control of any person's will. He seeks for our will to be in harmony with His will but not by any form of coercion. When many

Christians surrender "all to Jesus" they include their will. God will not take over the human will. We are free to make our own decisions at all times. Those who surrender their will may, unknowingly, surrender it to the control of unclean spirits who are waiting for that very opportunity. Under no circumstance should a believer surrender the will to any person or any thing.

Passivity, in many cases, is the consequence of a wrong concept of surrender to the Lord. There are those who believe if they surrender control of their mind to the Holy Spirit every thought will be motivated by the Holy Spirit. But God is not operating a divine puppet show. God needs followers who use their minds for decision making and carrying out the work of the kingdom. A non-working brain is of no value to God but it is a fertile ground for unclean spirits to work.

I have discussed the matter of hypnosis with a person who taught it in the medical field. Once he understood the principles of inner-healing and deliverance, he said, there is a level of hypnosis where unclean spirits are able to enter the sub-conscious mind. From there they would be able to influence all decision making. It is well to remember that God does not take control of your will but Satan will!

Control by a spirit of passivity results in mental inactivity when action is needed and activity when inactivity or reduced activity is desirable. There are those who find it difficult to differentiate between inactivity and passiveness. There are those periods of time when the mind does move into a state of apparent inactivity, at least at the conscious level. This is normal and a person is able to call the mind back into activity whenever necessary or desired. However, if a spirit of passivity is involved, the ability to control the activity of the mind is diminished. Persons suffering from such influence will frequently speak of feeling as if they have a band of iron around their head, of pressure within the head or of feeling a weight on the head. There is insomnia, loss of memory, inability to concentrate, indecisiveness and a lack of judgment.

When the imagination is invaded by passive spirits, it is as though it no longer remains under the control of the individual. Such a person is left to the deceitful works of unclean spirits who excite the imagination with visions and prophecies. What the person sees and hears is not based on objective reality but is only the manipulating of an open imagination. The thoughts are real; however, their source is the work of unclean spirits projected to the conscious mind in order to bring deception. To suggest to such a person that they have a wild imagination is folly for what they see and hear is a real vision or prophecy. But the source is not the Holy Spirit.

Beloved believe not every spirit, but try the spirits, whether they be of God: because many false prophets are gone out into the world. [I John 4:1]

This passage is concerned about false prophets and may be understood as testing the prophet. I do not believe it is a violation of the passage, though, to follow its admonition and test the spirit which may be inciting a person's imagination.

Perhaps you have met a person whose mind seems to be closed to all correction or teaching. A closed mind is a dangerous mind. Very often passive spirits close the mind so that further light and truth is completely shut out. Anyone attempting to instruct such a mind is regarded as ignorant or an intruder. Such a mind sees itself as being infallible and not to be questioned. To do so invites quick rebuttal or outright rejection.

In a similar but different manifestation the person will act and reason according to "super-natural commands" supposedly from God. When such commandments come the person will not examine them, believing that he/she is being led directly by God through visions, voices and scripture passages. Such a person is open to all sorts of suggestions and is led into bizarre activities in the name of Jesus Christ.

As passivity gains a foothold, lethargy and heaviness take over not only the mind but also the body and is manifested by a dullness in bodily function and attitude. A common symptom is the inability to look directly into another's eyes. Eye contact will be broken by a darting of the eyes from side to side. There may be a loss of elasticity in the body and a stooping of the back. As the whole person begins to fall into passivity, the faculties of the mind and body tend to become suppressed and, in some cases, dormant. As the spirits dictate, there may be a suppression of food, sleep and other normal activities. There may also be an awakening of the animalistic part of the carnal nature resulting in gluttony, wantonness and other base manifestations.

Bodily sensations must be monitored closely and not always interpreted as coming from the Holy Spirit. Any degree of invasion by unclean spirits may influence bodily sensations. It is easy to be deceived into becoming dominated by physical feelings, the sensual becomes the measure of spirituality. Every physical sensation, especially in the worship or praise setting, immediately becomes a spiritual experience. For instance, feelings of tingling, fire, cold, thrill or whatever are manifestations of the Holy Spirit. However, unclean spirits, the body and the mind are also capable of creating bodily sensations. Many Christians have been deceived into believing that such experiences in a Spirit-filled believer can only be from God, especially if occurring during worship and praise. It is unfortunate that so many are experiencing little more than sensual and/or emotional sensations.

Legal Ground

Before a Christian can be invaded by an unclean spirit there must be some means of allowing the spirit to enter. I have come to call that means "legal ground." Seeing spiritual warfare from a courtroom setting, the term is better understood.

Scripture speaks of Satan as the "accuser of the brethren (Rev. 12:9,10.)" As the accuser, he stands before God reciting every sin and weakness of the Christian, claiming his right to function. Those rights are based upon God's law. Jesus Christ, our Advocate (I John 2:1) pleads the cause of the sinner before the Father on the basis that He died for the sinner. The legal ground claimed by Satan lies in the area of willful and unrepented sin. Iniquity cannot go unresolved without becoming "legal ground" claimed by the accuser of the brethren.

The sin of unforgiveness provides one of the strongest legal grounds held by Satan. Many Christians overlook the impact which unforgiveness can have and fail to grasp its significance. It is not always the big trespasses but the smaller, seemingly insignificant occurrences, which wound but are soon forgotten and unforgiven. Often these become powerful areas in which the enemy may work. Our Lord understood this well:

> For if ye forgive men their trespasses, your heavenly Father will also forgive you: But if ye forgive not men their trespasses, neither will your Father forgive your trespasses. (Matt. 6:14-15) And when ye stand praying, forgive, if ye have ought against any: that your Father also which is in heaven may forgive you your trespasses. But if ye do not forgive, neither will your Father which is in heaven forgive your trespasses. [Mark 11:25,26]... forgive, and ye shall be forgiven." [Luke 6:37]

It has been our experience that many Christians are unaware they hold unforgiveness in their hearts. The incident has been covered over by time and been hidden in the sub-conscious mind. But whenever a similar incident occurs the old hurts are touched and a reaction sets in. That area of unforgiveness then becomes the legal ground for demonic activity. Most often unforgiveness is revealed by the Holy Spirit through the gifts of discernment, knowledge and/or wisdom.

Children often interpret events in a far different light than adults. Discipline, which may have been administered out of love and concern, often has been perceived as totally unjust by the child. A feeling of injustice may be followed by bitterness. As incident builds upon incident, over a period of time bitterness also grows. With maturity the individual may come to see the matter in its true nature, yet the unforgiveness and bitterness remain as legal ground for the enemy. Unless that legal ground is retaken through repentance, forgiveness and deliverance, the enemy will continue to claim his right to function.

Legal ground is given to the enemy whenever a Christian willfully sins.

> Neither give place to the devil ... Let no corrupt communication proceed out of your mouth ... grieve not the Holy Spirit ... Let all bitterness, and wrath, and clamor and evil speaking be put away from you, with all malice: [Eph.4:27,29-31]

When Paul says to not give any place to the devil, he is speaking to believers - those who know the Lord Jesus Christ. He knew full well that Christians could be careless in what they say and think. He also was aware that the enemy takes any advantage given to him. So he reminded his readers to not grieve the Holy Spirit. He is grieved whenever bitterness, wrath, evil speaking and malice is not put away. Any one of these constitutes legal ground for the enemy.

Legal ground is also given to the enemy by individuals who have not known the Lord Jesus Christ, whose lives for all practical purposes have served only the prince of this world. Upon accepting the Lord Jesus Christ there is no guarantee that the carnal mind and body will automatically be freed of all legal ground held by the enemy. The ground that was willfully given (out of ignorance, perhaps) must be retaken. Participation in witchcraft, the occult, sexual immorality, lying, cheating and other forms of wickedness all give ground to the enemy which he does not give up readily.

This is of utmost importance in parental relationships with children. The standards set by parents influence the choices of children. If God-pleasing standards are not set then one may expect ungodly standards will be set, opening the door to legal ground for Satan in the lives of the children. It is utter folly to take the position that the children be allowed to make their religious preference at maturity without any input from the parents in the childhood years. The enemy will use those years to infect their lives.

Legal ground is also claimed by the enemy in the area of the sins of the fathers. This must always be taken into consideration when breaking the enemies strongholds.

Sins Of The Fathers

Everyone comes into this world as an heir to an inheritance. Our forefathers and mothers have all left a legacy that is not material. In this ministry we are concerned with that spiritual legacy which awaits each birth. The lives lived by our ancestors play a significant role in our daily walk, even for Christians. That inheritance may be a blessing or a curse, depending upon the character of our ancestral linage.

When I first began to grasp the significance of this truth I gave serious thought to my own ethnic background. I had always been proud of my Scandinavian background and still hold a deep respect for my grandparents. They were honest, hard working, trustworthy people. The family line was steeped in Lutheran teachings and those standards produced good Christian stock. But as I looked back upon the ancestral lines I was also reminded that my Viking background was far from a peaceful one. No doubt some of my ancestors were involved in those periodic cruises to the coasts of England and other ports of call spreading ill-will as they sacked and plundered the cities. History records the violence of the Vikings and the fear that came into the hearts of the people they visited.

I knew of the prevailing tendency to explosive anger in many of the male members of the family line and how I had fought most of my life to control a violent rage within myself. I recalled the fear I lived with that some day I might lose control. Praise God, by breaking the curse of the fathers and through subsequent deliverance that rage is now gone. This is my testimony to the reality and importance of breaking the curse of the sins of the fathers.

There are pertinent Bible passages concerning the curse of the sins of the fathers.

> Thou shalt not bow thyself down to them, nor serve them: for I the Lord thy God am a jealous God, visiting the iniquity of the fathers upon the children unto the third and fourth generation of them that hate me. [Exodus 20:5-6]

> And the Lord passed by before him, and proclaimed, The Lord, the Lord God, merciful and gracious, longsuffering, and abundant in goodness and truth, keeping mercy for thousands, forgiving iniquity and transgression and sin, and that will by no means clear the guilty; visiting the iniquity of the fathers upon the children, and upon the children's children, unto the third and to the fourth generation. [Exodus 34:6-7]

> The Lord is longsuffering, and of great mercy, forgiving iniquity and transgression, and by no means clearing the guilty, visiting the iniquity of the fathers upon the children unto the third and fourth generation. [Numbers 14:18]

> Thou showest loving-kindness unto thousands, and recompensest the iniquity of the fathers into the bosom of their children after them: the Great, the Mighty God, The Lord of hosts, is his name, ... [Jeremiah 32:18]

> Our fathers have sinned, and are not; and we have borne their iniquities. [Lamentations 5:7]

> Therefore say unto the house of Israel, Thus saith the Lord God; Are ye polluted after the manner of your fathers? and commit ye whoredom after their abominations? [Ezekiel 20:30]

> And they that are left of you shall pine away in their iniquity in your enemies' lands; and also in the iniquities of their fathers shall they pine away with them. If they shall confess their iniquity, and the iniquity of their fathers, ... Then will I remember my covenant with Jacob, and also with my covenant with Isaac, and also my covenant with Abraham will I remember; and I will

125

remember the land. [Leviticus 26:39-42. See also vs. 36-38]

These passages are rather hard to reconcile to the love of God, yet here is established a principle of God, Who is unchangeable - the same yesterday, today and forever. The sins of one generation do have devastating effects on the succeeding ones. However, God is not angry with the succeeding generations nor is He punishing them for the previous generation's iniquity. If there is anger toward any, it is because of their own sins.

To understand the principle of generational curses you must first understand the attributes of God for that is where this whole matter is rooted. Most of us are familiar with the attributes of omnipotence, omnipresence and omniscience, which say God is all powerful, present in all places at the same time and all knowing. God is also unchangeable, just and will not ignore sin. His attribute of justice demands that sin be punished. Sin must be dealt with, either it is resolved or it will wreak its consequences. Sin left unconfessed, unrepented and unforgiven becomes the legal ground for satanic activity in generations to follow.

There are those who believe that Jesus Christ removed this principle. Let us look at the Bible passages used to support their belief.

Behold the days come, saith the Lord, that I will sow the house of Israel and the house of Judah with the seed of man, and with the seed of beast. And it shall come to pass that like as I have watched over them, to pluck up, and to break down, and to throw down, and to destroy, and to afflict; so will I watch over them, to build, and to plant, saith the Lord. In those days they shall say no more, The fathers have eaten a sour grape, and the children's teeth are set on edge. But every one shall die for his own iniquity: every man that eateth the sour grape, his teeth shall be set on edge. [Jeremiah 31:27-30]

What mean ye, that ye use this proverb concerning the land of Israel, saying, The fathers have eaten sour grapes, and the children's teeth are set on edge? As I live, saith the Lord God, ye shall not have occasion any more to use this proverb in Israel. Behold, all souls are mine; as the soul of the father, so also the soul of the son is mine: the soul that sinneth, it shall die. [Ezekiel 18:2-4]

The fathers shall not be put to death for the children, neither shall the children be put to death for the fathers: every man shall be put to death for his own sin. [Deuteronomy 24:16]

A basic principle of biblical interpretation is that all interpretation must remain true to the context from which the passage has been taken. The context for these three passages is sin and death, establishing that the ultimate fruit of sin is spiritual death. The residual effects of sin in the life of an individual or in the lives of his children and succeeding generations is not discussed.

The mind-set of the people of the Old Testament expected punishment for sin to follow rapidly the committing of sin. They also believed as the king went so went the nation and as the head of the family went so went the family. So then the saying: If the father ate sour grapes then the children's teeth would be set on edge. Through Ezekiel and Jeremiah God said they were no longer to use that old saying. He said a day was coming when the old adage would be completely out of order and each person was to face up to a neglected truth. This was not a new truth but is a reminder that from the very beginning each individual has been responsible for his or her own sin. The contemporaries of Ezekiel and Jeremiah had ignored the truth that no person is to die for another's sin, each person dies for his/her own sin.

The verses following the Ezekiel and Jeremiah passages quoted above speak very clearly to this point. Ezekiel cites the condition of those begotten by the fathers and the responsibility of those children to deal with their own sin. In Exodus, God speaks concerning the Second Commandment:

Thou shalt not make unto thee any graven image, or any likeness of anything that is in the heaven above, or that is in the earth beneath, or that is in the water under the earth: thou shalt not bow down thyself to them, nor serve them: for I the Lord thy God am a jealous God, visiting the iniquity of the fathers upon the children unto the third and fourth generation of them that hate me: and showing mercy unto thousands of them that love me, and keep my commandments. [Exodus 20:4-6]

Jeremiah repeats this Commandment, giving it added emphasis:

Thou showest loving-kindness unto thousands, and

recompensest the iniquity of the fathers into the bosom of their children after them: the Great, the Mighty God, the Lord of hosts, is his name, [Jeremiah 32:18]

Since the context of the passages cited is death (and not residual effects) they cannot be used to set aside the passages that refer to the sins of the fathers. The passages concerning breaking the curse of the sins of the fathers speak of the consequences of unresolved sin which affect the following generations. Satan exploits the results of iniquity using it as legal ground to harass and torment. The children cannot be put to death for that iniquity unless they fall into the same deception as did their fathers. Even though they should fall into the same iniquity, through confession and repentance they can be freed from the condemnation of death. Jesus Christ won that victory in His resurrection from the dead.

Note what was said in Jeremiah 32:18: something comes down into the very bosom of the children of following generations. Not only does the consequence come upon the children but also into their bosom or very being. But, once again, let it be understood that nobody dies for another's sin; each person is responsible for his own sin. However, the consequences of iniquity come upon and within the children and give legal ground for satanic activity.

In the Reality of Spiritual Warfare section of this book it was shown that Satan exploits the "sin principle" present in every man and woman. Viewing the descendants of Adam and Eve listed in scripture, a rather clear picture emerges of the progression of that principle. For instance, in tracing the descendants of Cain, the same rebellious attitude repeats itself in his descendants. A close review of the kings of Israel and Judah also reveals certain characteristics appearing generation after generation. One can scarcely look at the biblical record without noticing the repetitious acts of iniquity moving through the generations.

Practical experience in this ministry has shown us that evil influences move from one generation to another. Very often, when we ask the Holy Spirit to probe the deep recesses of the subconscious mind of a counselee, the source of the problem is traced to a previous generation. Even in cases of a traumatic event in the mother's womb (such as an attempted abortion or the consideration of abortion,) deeper probing may reveal that the action of the mother was prompted by a spirit of murder which has moved through the family lines. Again, a clear example of the generational curse is that of repeated alcoholism in certain families.

Our work with troubled Christians and the experiences they relate during deliverance sessions has led us to the conviction that at the very moment of conception the legacy of past generations is passed on to the new generation. The legal ground claimed by the enemy because of prior unconfessed iniquity opens the fetus to the influences of that sin. It is this influence or legal ground which is nullified through the breaking of the curse of the sins of the fathers.

Breaking the curse of the sins of the fathers is relatively easy. God, in His grace, makes provisions for that need. In both the Old and New Testaments God has set forth a principle for dealing with sin and iniquity. In I John 1:9 we are told, "If we confess our sins, he is faithful and just to forgive us our sins, and to cleanse us from all unrighteousness." That same principle also appears in the Old Testament.

> And ye shall perish among the heathen, and the land of your enemies shall eat you up. And they that are left of you shall pine away in their iniquity in your enemies' lands; and also in the iniquities of their fathers shall they pine away with them. If they shall confess their iniquity, and the iniquity of their fathers, with their trespass which they trespassed against me, and that also they have walked contrary to me;... Then will I remember my covenant with Jacob, and also my covenant with Isaac, and also my covenant with Abraham will I remember; and I will remember the land. [Leviticus 26:38-42]

The principles of confession, repentance, forgiveness and restoration break the curse of the sins of the fathers.

Since a generation falls somewhere within a thirty or forty year range it is virtually impossible for a person to know what iniquity may have occurred and gone unresolved. Four generations back would take a person today somewhere near the Civil War period. Very few people would have enough accurate knowledge of the family line to pin-point the exact sin. Furthermore, the curse of the bastard child extends to ten generations (Deut.23:2.) Therefore, we ask the Holy Spirit to take control of the imagination, conscious and subconscious mind of the counselee in order to probe the deep recesses of the memory.

In that probing by the Holy spirit those things which have worked as a curse are often brought to light. Whatever is revealed is confessed along with a listing of the manifestations of the works of the flesh drawn from Rom. 1:29-31; I Cor. 6:9-10 and Galatians 5:19. We know that the forefathers of the counselee have not been guilty of every manifestation of the works of the flesh but those of which they were guilty will have been confessed. Once sin is confessed, forgiveness is sought and accepted. Then the counselee, in the name of Jesus Christ, lifts every curse and iniquity that has come upon them and their children. [Note: Lest the accusation be made that this is praying for the dead, remember nothing is changed for the dead ancestors. They have been judged by the word of God and that cannot be changed by any man's prayer. The prayer is to gain the freedom of the counselee, his/her children and those yet to be born into that family line.]

Since a demonic strong man and his family have been able to enter because of this curse, after all curses have been lifted, the strong man and his family are commanded to leave the counselee. One may expect to see a mild manifestation with the departure of the strong man. In some cases nothing appears to happen. However, a person with the gift of discerning of spirits will sense if something has happened. Often the counselee will respond by saying they feel as though a heavy burden has been lifted. Seldom is there any violent manifestation.

I have been asked a number of times why it is necessary to confess the sins of one's ancestors. The thinking seems to be that "they sinned, not me." It is not necessary! No one, not even God, will demand it of you. But if you desire to be free of the bondages that curse brings upon you, do it God's way. It is God who says, "If they will confess their iniquities and the iniquities of their fathers ... (Lev. 26:39.)"

We find that breaking the power of the curse of the sins of the fathers makes the subsequent inner-healing and deliverance much easier to minister. Once the curse is broken specific problem areas are readied for ministry.

CHAPTER 8

WEAPONS OF WARFARE

Role of Spiritual Gifts

During a counseling session a person receiving ministry said to Shirley and me: "You must have been reading my mail." And so it must seem to those on the receiving end of the ministry of the gifts of the Spirit. Successful deliverance is totally dependent upon the gifting of the Holy Spirit to set the captives free.

This does not mean those ministering are merely puppets of the Spirit but, rather, there is a direct cooperation with the Spirit's leadership. Psychological and counseling skills must be secondary to the activity of the Holy Spirit.

> For to one is given by the Spirit the word of wisdom; to another the word of knowledge by the same Spirit; to another faith by the same spirit; to another the gift of healing by the same Spirit; to another the working of miracles; to another prophecy; to another discerning of spirits; to another divers tongues; to another interpretation of tongues; but all these worketh that one and the selfsame Spirit dividing to every man severally as he will. [1 Cor.12:8-11]

The most common of the gifts in deliverance ministry are those of wisdom, knowledge, healing and discerning. These may function separately or in conjunction with each other. While one or the other of the gifts may seem to predominate, it does not mean that the others are of lesser importance. All are needed for the fulfillment of Christ's ministry.

The gift of discerning, especially in Shirley's ministry, has been a strong aspect of our working as a team. While listed in the scripture as "discerning of spirits," it does not seem to be limited to that alone. Often there is a revelation of a particular area in the counselee's life or perhaps a defining of the root problem as well as the identification of particular spirits.

In a frequent manifestation of this gift, the discerner will have a mental picture accompanied by emotional and physical feelings. The picture and feelings may identify the problem or, when described, will bring to the mind of the counselee a memory which had been pushed out of the conscious level. It is not unusual for the counselee and the discerner to see and experience similar things simultaneously. On occasion, the discerner will see a mental picture of some object, usually black in color, attached to the brain or some other part of the counselee's anatomy. What is revealed is not always pleasant to behold but through such a gift the source of bondage is pin-pointed and deliverance follows.

This gift is especially useful in breaking the curse of the sins of the fathers. The lineage, whether maternal or paternal, through which the bondage has come will be revealed. The root problem itself may then be attacked.

It is interesting that the mental picture or thoughts will be in alignment with the context of the discerner's intellectual level or personality. It is not unusual for two persons to see widely divergent scenes, yet the basic message or principle will be in agreement between the two.

I have found the word of knowledge is the gift most often functioning in me during ministry. During the initial interview or while going through the preparatory prayer, a word will begin to dominate my thoughts. I have found that when I act on that word, even though there has been nothing to indicate a particular problem, the Holy Spirit has been faithful and an unclean spirit is revealed and then cast out.

The word of knowledge usually confirms the gift of discerning. When the mental picture of the discerner is related and not readily understood, a word will come that will bring immediate clarity and understanding as to how to proceed. This demonstrates, rather graphically, the necessity of the team ministry and how the spiritual gifts enhance each other.

The word of wisdom most often functions toward the end of a session when counsel is being given concerning how the bondage came and how its return can be prevented. It is wonderful to see a newly released person, confused as to how in their situation they can apply the principles to remain free, hear the word of wisdom and come to a full understanding of how to resist the enemy and stay free.

Many seem to be unsure of the difference between words of knowledge and wisdom. A simple principle may help. Knowledge has to do with information and facts while wisdom refers to the proper use of information and facts. Again, the working together of the gifts is evident: wisdom without information cannot function and knowledge without wisdom is useless.

Healing is essential to the full deliverance from demon invasion. The activity of unclean spirits within a person and the battle to free them will leave a person wounded in mind and body. These wounds can be healed through the ministry of the gifts of healing and should be expected. Prayer for healing must always accompany the prayer for deliverance. Jesus wants to heal the brokenhearted and the bruised.

All the gifts of the Spirit can and may function at any point during a session. The Holy Spirit cannot be tied to formulas or counseling techniques. He will use whomever He will, whenever He so chooses, in order to break bondages in the lives of God's people. Without the gifting of the Holy Spirit a counseling session will be an exercise in psychological counseling and the employment of learned counseling approaches. With the gifting of the Holy Spirit deliverance, healing and miracles will take place.

Please do not misunderstand what I am saying: I am not opposed to psychologists, psychiatrists or other counselors just as I am not opposed to medical doctors. Modern psychiatry has become very adept at diagnosing the root problems of many sufferers. However, accurate diagnosis does not effect a cure. And when the root problem is of the spiritual realm, it takes spiritual means to bring about full healing.

So it is we must be careful to utilize spiritual means to bring about spiritual deliverance. To fail in this is to leave the victim in bondage and the minister in frustration. God has given us the most effective means possible in the gifts of the Spirit. These spiritual weapons will discover and engage the enemy of our souls and we shall overcome!

Sense Of The Spirit

I once heard a man say, "Each of us, through experience, develop the five bodily senses of sight, hearing, smell, feeling and taste. However, few truly develop a sense of the spirit." I was intrigued by that statement because at the time I was seeking for an awareness of the leading of the Holy Spirit in my own life. I was finding it most difficult to determine the source of the thought patterns which would flow through my mind. This was especially true if they were accompanied by bodily sensations such as tingling, heat, cold or unusual emotional responses. I seemed to lack a sense of when my own spirit wanted to exercise control over the five natural senses in order to impart information or give direction. I am convinced that many Christians easily fall into deception because they have not yet developed a sense of the spirit.

If the created man is spirit, soul and body, which I believe and teach, then there must be a functioning of each part of this tri-partite person. We understand the function between the soul (intellect, will, emotions) and the body. When any one of the five bodily sensors (eye, ear, etc.) receives an impression, it is immediately passed on to the soul to be evaluated by the intellect, responded to by the will and/or reacted to by the emotions. This same kind of sensing should exist between the spirit and the soul.

Just as the body inhabits the world and brings to the soul the facts of that realm, the spirit inhabits the spiritual realm and brings to the soul spiritual realities. In the unregenerate person that sense is undeveloped and the soul is without the input of the spirit. When a person receives Jesus Christ as Savior, the spirit is made alive and again responsive to the things of the Spirit. The sensory part of the human spirit needs development and growth so the soul can be guided by the Holy Spirit. Guidance is communicated to the soul through the sense of the spirit, a sixth sense, if you will.

The activity of the sense of the spirit takes place between the human spirit and human mind, not between the Holy Spirit and the mind separate from the human spirit. While it is true that the Holy Spirit in fills and energizes the human spirit it is the human spirit which transmits spiritual understanding to the individual. The Holy Spirit imparts faith, wisdom and knowledge to the human spirit which then brings this to bear upon the soul of the believer.

There does not appear to be any Scriptural evidence to indicate the Holy Spirit is given control of a person's will, mind or body. To the contrary the Holy Spirit's role appears to be that of a teacher or imparter of faith, wisdom and knowledge.

> Howbeit when he, the Spirit of truth, is come, he will guide you into all truth: for he shall not speak of himself; but whatsoever he shall hear, that shall he speak: and he will show you things to come. He shall glorify me: for he shall receive of mine, and shall show it unto you. [John 16:13-14]

That imparting takes place in the believer's spirit and then flows into the mind of the believer as he/she opens to that process.

It is at this very point that the sense of the spirit becomes of vital importance. The root activity of the sense of the spirit is to judge or examine all incoming information flowing into the mind. Paul seems to speak to this:

> ...the natural man receiveth not the things of the Spirit of God: for they are foolishness unto him: neither can he know them, because they are spiritually discerned. But he that is spiritual judgeth all things... [I Cor.2:14-15]

So then, the sense of the spirit begins with knowledge of the Word of God which is the measuring rod for judging or examining that which comes to the mind of the believer. Spiritual thoughts must not be assumed to be true. They must stand the test of the Word of God before being received and acted upon. Religious assumptions must always give way before the Word of God.

The Holy Spirit speaks only the things He hears from the Godhead and things which glorify the Lord Jesus Christ. He does not override a person's will and take control of the mind. Paul said the "things of the Spirit of God" cannot be received by the natural man, for they are spiritually discerned. That is, they flow from the spirit of man into the renewed mind which has the knowledge to judge and examine all incoming information.

The sense of the spirit, simply put, is the awareness of truth which grows and develops in the renewed mind of the believer. That awareness enables the believer to judge between the specificity of absolute truth and the counterfeit of the enemy. A passive mind assumes it hears the truth whereas a renewed, spirit directed mind judges and examines all it receives.

Awareness can come only as the believer heeds the words of Paul:

> ... put off concerning the former conversation the old man, which is corrupt according to deceitful lusts; and be renewed in the spirit of your mind; and that ye put on the new man, which after God is created in righteousness and true holiness. [Eph. 4:22-24]

Binding and Loosing

In many deliverance ministries the enemy is allowed to dictate the course of the sessions. When deliverance ministers allow violence, cursing, vomiting and other intense demonstrations I believe the enemy is dictating the course of action and, to a degree, is in control of the session. If this is permitted, the enemy will use the opportunity to glorify and call attention to itself.

When we first came into this ministry the enemy did dictate what would happen. Because of this we were exposed to violence and the wrath of the unclean spirits. Shirley and I were spit upon, torn by fingernails, struck with fists, kicked at, wrestled to the floor, called the most vile names and suffered many other indignities. It seemed that if we could outlast the unclean spirit it would leave due to exhaustion only to be replaced by another demon until there seemed to be no end to the procession of spirits.

It was for this very reason that we sought the Lord for guidance as to how we might gain control of the sessions. Again the Holy Spirit led us into the scriptures.

.... whatsoever ye shall bind on earth shall be bound in heaven: and whatsoever ye shall loose on earth shall be loosed in heaven. [Matt. 18:18]

And I will give unto thee the keys of the kingdom of heaven: and whatsoever thou shalt bind on earth shall be bound in heaven: and whatsoever thou shalt loose on earth shall be loosed in heaven. [Matt.16:19]

Let the high praises of God be in their mouth, and a two edged sword in their hand; to execute vengeance upon the heathen, and punishment upon the people: to bind their kings with chains, and their nobles with fetters of iron; to execute upon them the judgment written; this honor have all his saints. Praise ye the Lord. [Psalm 149:6-9]

Far above all principality and power, and might, and dominion, and every name that is named, not only in this world, but also in that which is to come: and hath put all things under his feet, ... [Eph. 1:21,22]

Or else how can one enter into a strong man's house, and spoil his goods, except he first bind the strong man? and then he will spoil his house. [Matt. 12:29; Mark 3:27]

The authority and power to deal with unclean spirits transcends the earthly and extends to heaven itself. Note what is said in the Matthew 16 passage, ". . . whatsoever thou shalt bind on earth shall be bound in heaven: and whatsoever thou shalt loose on earth shall be loosed in heaven." The very thought of such authority should cause one to stand in awe. It is never to be taken lightly.

Binding and loosing cannot be properly understood apart from Christian authority and should be utilized within that context. In our counseling ministry we exercise this authority daily. We have come to see that utilizing the keys to bind and loose are essential in spiritual warfare.

The original language of scripture interprets binding as: to gird, to wrap, to fetter, to tie, to press or compress, to entangle, to yoke, to fasten or to obligate. The child of God has the God-given authority and power to restrict, place fetters upon, yoke, entangle, tie, or in any other manner obligate unclean spirits to the obedience of that authority.

Unclean spirits are bound in order to prevent any hindering of the work of the Holy Spirit during the sessions. The most apparent evidence of this hindering work is confusion between those involved in the conduct of the deliverance ministry. Through access to human minds and wills, unclean spirits cause doubt, unbelief and confusion to be triggered in the minds of the counselee and/or counselor. This then hinders the work of the Holy Spirit. Therefore, every effort is made to curtail the work of unclean spirits. They are only as powerful as we allow them to be and can only function to the degree allowed in our minds and bodies.

Since the nature of unclean spirits is to find a vulnerable person to attack, the movement of unclean spirits is also restricted through binding. In prayer, any movement of unclean spirits is bound to that place where Jesus Christ wills they shall go.

The decision to send the unclean spirits to that place willed by Jesus Christ came about because of the conflicting views of various writers and ministers. Some would say to send them to the dry places; some to the pit; some to Hades and some to other very bizarre places. When we asked the Lord about this the answer was to command them to go wherever Jesus Christ willed they should go.

Likewise, unclean spirits are prevented from returning to the counselee, ourselves or any other person or place. Through prayer, the heavenly father is asked to assign holy angels to assure that all bindings are in place and that any other needed bindings be placed upon all unclean spirits. So then, all violence is bound, not only in the place of the sessions, but also in every place and person represented by the presence of the counselee.

In scriptural language loosing means to draw off, cast or shake off, open, make inactive, let go, lift up or lead forth. You will note that loosing is not restricted to loosing something from heaven nor is it restricted to loosing upon earth. The believer has authority to loose the hold of unclean spirits upon men, women and children and to actually loose and cast out, off or away.

Jesus says that whatsoever we desire, we may ask for, believing that it will be given, and we shall receive. This, then, must include opening the doors of heaven that blessings might flow down upon those for whom we intercede. It might be for the release of ministering angels, healing, knowledge or whatever. Again, we must recognize the awesomeness of this promise and never deal with it in a frivolous manner.

There are times when an unclean spirit will persevere in refusing to leave. Even through the legal ground has been dealt with and, to the best of our knowledge, none remains, the spirit still perseveres. On occasions I will ask the heavenly Father to loose the fire of His wrath upon such a spirit because it is defying the name of Jesus and trampling His blood underfoot. Sometimes the spirit will cry out, "Fire, fire, burning, burning!" and leave the person.

Loosing the power of the blood of Jesus Christ against unclean spirits serves, in many cases, to dislodge a stubborn spirit. We remind the unclean spirit that it is responsible for the shedding of that blood and that it cannot stand against the power of that blood. As the power of the blood is spoken of repeatedly the unclean spirit will usually leave.

When commanding unclean spirits to depart from a person we cut and loose all means whereby they have bound the counselee. We command that the person be loosed as well as cast the spirit out. We always ask that healing, peace and restoration be loosed from heaven on behalf of those to whom we have ministered.

Binding and loosing are to be perceived as tools of spiritual warfare available to the believer. Through these tools the child of God is enabled to overthrow and defeat the destructive work of the enemy among fellow Christians.

> For though we walk in the flesh, we do not war after the flesh: (for the weapons of our warfare are not carnal, but mighty through God to the pulling down of strongholds;) casting down imaginations, and every high thing that exalteth itself against the knowledge of God, and bringing into captivity every thought to the obedience of Christ. [II Cor. 10:3-5]

Ministering Angels

I recently heard a well known mass-media minister say that angels may be easily distinguished from unclean spirits (demons) by the fact that angels have bodies and the unclean spirits do not. That statement shocked me into the realization of how little is actually known and taught concerning the angelic realm.

The Church, especially in recent times, has done little teaching on the nature and activity of angels. Many Christians find their knowledge of angels limited to the appearances at the birth of the Christ Child and at His tomb immediately following the resurrection.

In my teaching sessions, there are always some who question that we ask the Heavenly Father to assign angels to carry out certain tasks on our behalf. We feel that the Holy spirit led us to request angelic help in our counseling ministry but, with that leading, it became necessary to ascertain if there was scriptural support for so doing. It is my desire to share what I have learned from scripture concerning the nature and work of angels.

Scripture seems to be rather clear that God created the angels as spirit-beings capable of manifesting their presence in human form. In Psalm 104, the psalmist reviews the work of the Creator and in the fourth verse says: "Who maketh his angels spirits; . . . ." In the first chapter of Hebrews the writer quotes the psalmist and then closes that chapter by saying:

Are they not ministering spirits, sent forth to minister for them who shall be heirs of salvation? [Heb. 1:14]

An angel appeared to Gideon, sat under an oak and spoke to him. To establish that he was more than human, the angel took the staff that was in his hand and touched the food that Gideon prepared. There arose a flame out of the rock which consumed the meal and then the angel disappeared (Judges 6.)

The childless parents of Samson, was visited by an angel who said the woman would conceive and bear a son. The husband, Manoah, did not realize he was talking to an angel. He offered the angel food and tried to get acquainted but the angel refused the food and would not reveal his name. Manoah then offered up a burnt sacrifice to God and the angel of the Lord ascended in the flame of the altar (Judges 15.)

There are significant insights in these two accounts concerning the angels. Angels appear in human form and so normally human that people do not recognize them for what they really are. They often perform some supernatural feat in order to establish their credentials. But their most common action is to deliver a message from God.

Angels are the servants of the most high God and are most often sent as His emissaries. In fact, that is exactly what they are called in both the Hebrew and Greek texts of the Bible. The word "angel" has been taken into the English language almost without change. This word, if translated, would mean "messenger, emissary, ambassador."

There are many examples throughout scripture to demonstrate this activity by angels.

1. The prophets Elijah, Daniel and Zachariah.

2. Concerning the birth of Jesus - Zachariah (John the Baptist's father,) Mary, Joseph and the shepherds.

3. In the early church - Philip the evan gelist, Cornelius the Roman centu- rion and Paul.

4. The revelation of John was shown by an angel.

However, the work of angels is by no means limited to carrying messages.

1. Angels visited destruction on Sodom and Gomorrah and protected Lot and his family from the wickedness of the inhabitants of Sodom.

2. When Elisha and his servant were threatened by the army of the king of Israel, in order to allay the fears of the servant Elisha asked that they be allowed to see into the spirit realm. They saw angels encircling them to protect them from the army.

3. Apparently angels accompanied Elijah into heaven (2 Kings 2:11-12.)

4. Loyal angels warred with the rebelling angels eventually casting them and Lucifer from heaven, contended for the body of Moses and withstood the satanic power over Persia when it attempted to stop a message getting to Daniel.

5. Hagar and Ishmael were given water by an angel and angels "ministered" to Jesus after His temptation.

6. The mouths of lions were stopped from destroying Daniel and Peter was delivered from prison by angels.

7. Angels transport the dead to their eternal habitation (Luke 16:22.)

8. All the prophets given vision of the throne of God tell of the angelic hosts constantly worshipping and praising God.

In our own day there have been numerous reports by sincere Christians of angelic appearances. Some report angels appearing at times of great danger averting an impending tragedy. It is difficult to dismiss such reports (though one may question and wonder) since scripture seems to ascribe these kind of activities to the angelic host.

The angels have no problem conversing with men and women. On at least one occasion an angel conversed with both man and God during the same appearance. In their conversations with men and women it seems the angels are reluctant to reveal their names. No explanation is offered but perhaps the Lord, in His infinite wisdom, knew that a first name familiarity might easily lead to evil worship or veneration of the angels. Scripture is clear that this is a serious possibility:

> Let no man beguile you of your reward in a voluntary
> humility and worshipping of angels .... [Col. 2:18]

This is further confirmed by the angel telling John not to worship him:

> ... see thou do it not: for I am thy fellow servant, and of
> thy brethren the prophets, and of them which keep the
> sayings of this book. [Rev. 22:9]

It has become rather clear that the angels minister to and for the people of God. It would seem that Christians have failed to utilize the ministering work of the angels. It is true that some, in the New Testament era, have learned to call upon the angelic host. By the leading of the Holy Spirit, we have learned to ask the Heavenly Father to assign angels to various tasks in our behalf. A word of caution is in order. Angels are fellow servants with us and are not to be commanded or ordered by Christians. Rather, they are under the direct command of the Father so it is to Him we direct our petition.

God has set before us wonderful ministering gifts in the person of the angels. May we learn to call upon the Lord for the release of these ministries in the Church of today.

Inner-Healing

It is important that inner-healing and deliverance be seen as distinct, though closely interrelated, aspects of ministry. Deliverance involves the identifying of unclean spirits indwelling a person and the casting out of the same. Inner-healing involves the identifying of problem areas, usually a result of traumatizing experiences of the past, and then correcting the situation.

Those involved in the inner-healing ministry usually seek a probing of the sub-conscious mind by the Holy Spirit. Once the problem area has been brought to the conscious level by the Holy Spirit (most often a mental picture of an incident) the counselee is led through a healing experience. It is at this point the method used becomes important.

In the "Directive Method," used by many counselors, the purpose is to give the counselee a pleasant counterpart to the traumatic experience. The counselee, either through direct memory or by the help of the Holy Spirit, will have a describable mental picture of the traumatic event. The person is directed to "invite" or "see" Jesus Christ come into the picture. Then a step-by-step correcting of the situation follows. Once the desirable experience has occurred the Holy Spirit is requested to seal this into the memory of the counselee thereby healing the wounds the person received from the bad experience.

Some counselors suggest the counselee picture something especially comfortable and pleasing such as a walk beside a beautiful lake. Then the counselee is led in a prayer to replace the hurting experience with the pleasant one. For some this may be sufficient to free them from the continuing consequences of the original bad experience. However, it is our experience that many who have gone through this method still suffer the consequences of past traumatic experiences.

There are two problem areas with the Directive Method. The first is the counselor giving step-by-step directives as to what mental picture should be seen by the counselee. The same thing can be accomplished by post-hypnotic suggestion. Psychiatrists use similar directive methods. If there is to be a lasting healing, it will come through the healing power of the Lord Jesus Christ - free of human direction.

Secondly, directive inner-healing may serve to erase some of the hurts and wounds but not deal with the root problem. More often than some suspect, an unclean spirit may have become involved with the person at the time of the trauma. If that spirit is not cast out, little more than band-aid healing will occur. The root of the problem must be dealt with before there can be total healing. Until the unclean spirit has left, the afflicted person will likely continue to be hurt and hurting others.

The Holy Spirit has led Shirley and I into a non-directive approach to inner-healing. The Holy Spirit is asked to bring the troubling incident to the conscious level. When the counselee affirms the incident is in mind, the Lord Jesus Christ is asked to enter into that scene and manifest His presence to the counselee. When it is determined that this has occurred, the Lord is asked to correct whatever needs correcting in the incident and to heal the wounds in the memory. Time is allowed by the counselors for the Lord to minister the necessary healing with no interruptions.

Often the counselee may indicate that the Lord is present in the perimeters of the incident but does not enter into the situation. It is then necessary to determine if there is unforgiveness or some other sin which needs to be dealt with before a healing can be effected. By the gift of discernment, a counselor frequently sees the same picture as the counselee. This, combined with the word of knowledge or wisdom, usually reveals the reason preventing healing by the Lord Jesus Christ. The work of the enemy is clearly seen, repentance and/or deliverance is effected and healing is accomplished.

It is important that those who feel called to minister in the areas of inner-healing and deliverance understand that inner-healing and deliverance are closely interrelated. If there has been a wounding of the mind, accompanied with painful memories, there is need for inner-healing. If unclean spirits have been exploiting the wound, they must be dealt with and inner-healing should then be ministered. In every case where unclean spirits have been cast out, inner-healing must be ministered.

Far too often, those involved in these ministries see themselves in separate and conflicting work. This must end. If those working in the inner-healing ministry fail to discern the presence of unclean spirits and such are not cast out, the problem will continue and probably worsen. On the other hand, when demons are cast out and inner-healing not administered, the footholds for the devil often remain and the end result will be worse than before ministry.

These ministries are complimentary and must be worked together. The Lord Jesus Christ has called us to peace and nowhere is this more necessary than in the inner-healing and deliverance ministry.

CHAPTER 9

DOING BATTLE

Having examined the variety of weapons available to believers with which to engage the enemy it is now time to begin the engagement. The following material relates to private individual counseling sessions.

The Counseling Session

The session usually begins with general conversation designed to establish rapport with the counselee. If this is the first time for the counselee then you are probably strangers and a foundation of trust needs to be built. We have found that the simple question, "Why are you here?", often opens the door to the needs of the individual. This also discovers whether the person came freely or was coerced by well-meaning but unwise friends or relatives.

Early in the session the counselor should probe the counselee's relationship with the Lord Jesus Christ. Is the person genuinely converted? Has he/she been baptized in (filled with) the Holy Spirit? Is there submission to the Lordship of Jesus Christ? If positive answers are not given to these questions one should hesitate to enter into inner-healing and deliverance with that person. The counselee needs to make a commitment of submission to the Lord Jesus Christ as a prerequisite for ministry. Should it be evident that such is not the case, it is appropriate to lead him/her into receiving Jesus as Savior and Lord.

It is advisable to obtain and keep written records of the person's background. Frequently areas of bondage are indicated by such a history. It is also wise to keep a running account of the sessions. Many times the Holy Spirit will lead the counselor back into these records in subsequent sessions. Not only is the counselor's memory renewed, it keeps one from needless repetition.

All areas of birth and growing up should be explored. Childhood relationships with parents, siblings and school friends are areas where the enemy may have made inroads into the person's life. Spiritual experiences should be recorded. The whole occult scene - seances, psychic healing, automatic writing, curses, hexes and the other occult practices - opens the mind and body to unclean spirits. Likewise, excursions into witchcraft such as ouija board, water-witching, fortune telling, table lifting and the like (even the slightest exposure) often opens one to the demonic realm. Today's popular occult games have left some participants incapacitated because of demon harassment. This whole area of a persons life needs to be explored and shared by the leading of the Holy Spirit.

Repeated, habitual, uncontrolled sin patterns are open doors to demonic activity. Incest has been prevalent in some family lines for generations because of the fear that exposing it would bring shame and guilt to the victim. The enemy can use this to destroy marriages through all sorts of sexual problems which often persist in subsequent generations. These following generations may not be guilty of the sin yet suffer the consequences of promiscuity, frigidity, homosexuality, sexual dysfunction, disrupted menstrual cycles and the like.

The drug scene is bad news for all who become involved. Confusion is a prominent liability, especially when the person becomes interested in the things of God. There is often severe memory loss and emotional problems which show up later in life. Many share with us that prior to their entry into drugs they possessed high academic abilities and after coming out of drug control they were never able to recapture that ability. Here again, all involvement with drugs must be shared if spiritual freedom is to be gained for the counselee.

The history of a person's health often reveals strongholds of demonic activity. Allergic reactions, frequent accidents, repeated illnesses all may point to a death spirit or other equally unwanted messengers of Satan. It is important to discover repeated health problems from generation to generation. This would include alcoholism, mental illness, heart and respiratory "weaknesses" and any other recurring patterns of death and sin.

It is important to probe into such areas because each is a field in which the demonic realm seeks to function. Sharing in the opening session serves to declare the grounds of warfare and allows the person to confess before the heavenly Father and to declare to Satan that the use of those sins is no longer to be considered legal ground!

Once the background history has been gathered it is well to determine the counselee's understanding of inner-healing and deliverance. Most come into the setting unaware of the mechanics involved. It must be understood that the counselor will not be shocked or disgusted by any revelations or actions of the counselee during the session and that all things are kept in strict confidence. The counselee needs to be aware that violence is controlled by angels commissioned for that purpose by the heavenly Father.

Freedom from bondage is dependent upon the willingness of the counselee to trust the counselor. It is the counselor's responsibility to possess the knowledge, experience and faith in the Lord Jesus Christ to merit that trust. As counselors, we must be aware of that responsibility and understand the necessity of total dependence upon the leading of the Holy Spirit. We are dealing with a person's personality and that's an awesome responsibility. Many times we are called upon to delve into areas that may completely alter the life-style and course of a person's life. The counselor must instill hope for healing and faith in the delivering work of Jesus Christ.

The people who come to us for ministry request that we minister to them. We do not now, nor have we ever, solicited counselees. The ministry is known through "word-of-mouth" advertising. Therefore, there is an element of trust already established. It is the counselors responsibility to nurture that trust. Every person entering this ministry must recognize the responsibility involved and the integrity it requires. It is not a ministry of fun and games, it is spiritual warfare. Souls and bodies are involved and there must be respect for the truth and a willingness to be led by the Holy Spirit. The counselee is entitled to know that this is the case before submitting to ministry.

It is also important that the counselee understand his/her role in the counseling sessions and what are the expectations of the counselor. All that should be expected of the counselee is agreement, cooperation and complete honesty with the counselor. Any attempt to cover up activities in any area grieves the Holy Spirit and causes the ministry gifts to cease functioning during a session. Confession and repentance will bring a restoration of ministry.

Often people come for counseling who have been counseled by psychiatrists and have learned to play the question and answer games of psychiatry. They have learned to give the answer which will please the counselor. In this ministry there is no such need because there are no right or wrong questions and answers with which to play games. Freedom from demonic activity and control comes through the work of the Holy Spirit as He brings the authority of the name of Jesus Christ and the power of His shed blood to bear against demonic forces. An honest sharing and confession of experiences and feelings is the opening step to freedom.

It is not uncommon for people to come for ministry fearing there might be violence if there is some kind of demonic bondage. In our ministry violence is the exception, not the rule. The Lord has graciously led us into a relatively non-violent deliverance ministry. Since violence is restricted and, in most cases, not in evidence, there is little that may happen to bring embarrassment to the counselee.

The counselee should be encouraged to relax and follow the leadership of the counselor. The counselee is urged not to use a prayer language or to be speaking praise to the Lord during the session. The speech and thought faculties of the counselee are needed for unclean spirits to manifest. Time can be given at the close of a session for worship and praise.

The next step is the preparatory prayer. It is recommended that each counselor become aware of needs and develop their own prayer but the model prayer pinpoints the pertinent areas of concern and may be used as is. Improper preparation can open the door for the enemy to exploit the session and waste valuable time. The enemy will use any opportunity to glorify himself. Therefore, the preparatory prayer is important in that it binds his activities from the very beginning of the session. The counselee may not understand what is being done. However, the counselor must not become concerned about this but take responsibility to set the captive free with the least show of force and in the shortest period of time.

Preparatory Prayer

A crucial part in deliverance sessions is the preparatory prayer. The model preparatory prayer found at the end of this section has gone through several changes. At first, the prayer tended to be long and rather detailed in nature. Not understanding our authority in Christ, we pleaded with God for protection in every area we felt the enemy might attack. We feared that unclean spirits might enter or attach themselves to us when deliverance was attempted. Instead of binding the demons, we would plead fearfully with God to protect us from mental and/or physical retaliation.

As we began to see our God-given authority and strengths as believers in the Lord Jesus Christ, we became aware that many of the things we were asking the Lord to do were actually in our area of responsibility and authority. Thus, more and more we began to exercise our authority and dropped the elements that pleaded for protection.

Respect for the wiles of the enemy is retained but the elements of fear have been discarded. The present prayer contains the elements we feel are essential. However, each person, led by the Holy Spirit, should develop the prayer they feel they can best use in faith.

We ask the heavenly Father to assign holy angels to fill the building and property where the sessions are to take place. Early experiences convinced us the enemy will react to spiritual warfare with physical harassment and even violence toward property or persons. Often counselees, not knowing what can take place, have not prayed for protection for their families or circumstances. Therefore, we ask that divine protection include all loved ones and circumstances represented by our involvement and the person of the counselee. This is not from personal fear but to insure the enemy will not be free to retaliate.

Next is the binding of all unclean spirits. Because of the importance of understanding the binding and loosing as part of the weapons at our disposal, I have included a full explanation later in this part of the book. Suffice it to say here, we learned to bind all violence, not only in the place of the sessions but also in every place and person represented by the presence of the counselee.

It is our desire and choice that all thoughts, decisions and actions during a session be in agreement with the perfect will and mind of the Lord Jesus Christ and so we state it in the prayer. There is always the possibility of falling into error and unknowingly serve the purposes of the enemy. Therefore, we trust the Holy Spirit to stop us, correct us or grant us discernment to see and understand the error and to correct it. We know that the enemy will use every opportunity to discredit the name of Jesus Christ. There must be open and total commitment to the guidance of the Holy Spirit.

The next portion of the preparatory prayer came as the result of a personal experience. I was requested to minister to a man who had maligned me and the ministry. He wreaked havoc against the ministry and the effects of his attacks are still surfacing many years later. I had dismissed the man from my mind by asking the Lord to forgive him and to forgive me for my bitterness. When he later requested ministry I felt all of the resentment and bitterness rise up within me. I knew that my flesh would not allow me to minister effectively to him. I met with him, forgave him to the best of my ability and set down the requirements to be met before I would minister to him. He was told that if he fulfilled those requirements another session would be arranged. In my own mind I was convinced he would never meet the requirements.

The next time I came into the city in which he lived his name was the first on the list for counseling. I knew I could not minister to this man with the turmoil that still stirred within me. What was I to do? (I know there are those who will glibly say, "just forgive him," but there are those times when forgiveness is nearly impossible.)

The night before he was scheduled for counseling I sought the Lord for answers. I confessed my inability to bring my flesh under control and I pleaded that somehow the Lord might love the man through me in spite of my flesh. I received no immediate direction but was awakened in the middle of the night with the thought I should read Ezekiel 42:14:

> When the priests enter therein, then shall they not go out of the holy place into the outer court, but there shall lay their garments wherein they minister, for they are holy: and shall put on other garments, and shall approach unto those things which are for the people.

I puzzled over the passage for a considerable period of time. I knew the Lord was saying something to me but I could not grasp what it was. Suddenly, this thought moved through my mind:

> Why are you so slow to understand when I speak to you? If the priest is to take off his garments because they are holy and put on others to minister the common things, should he not first put on holy garments to enter the holy place?

I was stunned. How could I expect to minister if I could not put off the earthly to take on the holy? I also realized only the Holy Spirit could bring it about - I did not know how but I knew the Holy Spirit did! I would trust Him. At the beginning of the session the next day I prayed:

> Father, You know the condition of my heart and the power of my flesh. I cannot minister this day without Your love. I ask now that everything of my humanity and flesh that would hinder the flow of Your love be stripped away by the Holy Spirit. Allow me now to take on the priestly garments, to come into the center of the holy place of Your will. Grant to me to draw from all You have to give to me.

As I began to minister to the man I suddenly realized love was flowing out from me to him. I could not believe what was happening. I even tried to express anger toward the man but none came. I knew what I had asked had come to pass. That prayer has been incorporated into the preparatory prayer to gain that same openness in all situations.

The next element of the prayer may seem to be off base to some so, once again, I cite a personal experience to explain its source. While ministering to a college professor, he complained that, whenever I commanded an unclean spirit to leave, a roaring sound exploded within his mind. The sound was so intense that it brought total confusion to him and he could not bring his will to agree with the ministry against the unclean spirit. The net result was total confusion for all involved.

I prayed for guidance. Immediately a thought came into my mind: "Ask the heavenly Father to assign angels to stand as a barrier between the conscious and subconscious mind of the man." I was perplexed. How can angels cause a division between the conscious and subconscious mind? There is an old saying about the "only game in town" and this seemed to be the "only game" in this situation. I asked the heavenly Father for the assignment of angels. I again commanded the unclean spirit to manifest. It was soon cast out. The man said the roaring was gone and the confusion stopped immediately.

I was concerned about continuing to ask for angels to divide the conscious and subconscious mind of a counselee. It just seemed too far-out and there was no need to provide more ammunition for the critics since the deliverance ministry already was subject to attack. No matter what I tried, though, nothing else produced the desired results. The elimination of confusion on the part of the counselee was desirable so I continued to ask that angels be assigned to that task.

We have found it expedient to close every possible means of communication between the satanic forces. In the authority of the name of Jesus Christ, the power of His shed Blood and the wielding of the Sword of The Spirit (God's Holy Word) we seek to sever and close communication in the evil realm. Communication between unclean spirits present in the counseling area with the principalities, powers, rulers of darkness in this world and spiritual wickedness in high places assigned to the local geographic area is severed and closed. Likewise communication with witches covens, occult workers and satanic workers of both the black and white arts is severed and closed. Communication between unclean spirits and Satan himself is severed and closed. Family and other familiar spirits are bound and commanded out of the counseling area. We ask the heavenly Father to assign angels to assure all these bindings are in place and to maintain them.

151

Prayer is a powerful and effective weapon in our ongoing warfare to establish the kingdom of God and to liberate Satan's captives. We do not pray to remind God of His promises nor to stimulate Him to action. It is we who need reminding and stimulation. Prayer brings us into agreement with the purposes of God and keeps us mindful of our absolute dependency upon the Lord. It saves us from our tendency to pride and ritual. Prayer is not the incantation of magic formulae but the calling upon the resources of Heaven. With such resources at hand, we know we have the victory. Never neglect prayer as an integral part of deliverance.

Manifestation

Most who come for inner-healing or deliverance do so with serious misconceptions. With sensational media presentations, horror books and a generally "bad press" most people are genuinely confused concerning true deliverance. In addition, many have had bad experiences in so-called deliverance sessions. When these incidents are embellished by vivid imaginations a person's expectations can be rather bizarre and many come fearing the manifestations that may occur during a session.

There is a tendency to associate deliverance with exorcism and works of magic and/or witchcraft. Exorcism is related to curses; deliverance is a casting away of the unclean spirits in the name and authority of the Lord Jesus Christ. It is an authority that all believers can walk in.

What is meant by manifestations? The American College Dictionary definition of manifest:

> 1. readily perceived by the eye or understanding; evident; obvious; apparent; plain: a manifest error. 2. psychoanal. apparent or disguising [used of conscious feelings and ideas which conceal and yet incorporate unconscious ideas and impulses]: the manifest content of a dream as opposed to the latent content which it conceals. 3. to make manifest to the eye or the understanding; show plainly. 4. to prove; put beyond doubt or question ...

Manifestation is defined:

1. Act of manifesting.
2. State of being manifested.
3. A means of manifesting; indication.
4. A public demonstration as for political effect.
5. Spiritualism. a materialization.

Using this definition, a manifestation of demonic activity during a deliverance session is some activity by or within the counselee which is perceivable to the eye or understanding of the counselor. It will be evident or apparent to any person observing. There will be a visible demonstration which gives evidence that something is happening within the counselee. The manifestation may occur at the conscious level in response to a command by the counselor or at an unconscious level (at least to the counselee.) The manifestations may be slight or exaggerated in nature. An experienced counselor will detect even the lightest manifestation and not be distracted by the exaggerated demonstrations.

There can be a manifestation by an unclean spirit which will conceal or disguise its true nature. For instance, there may be a manifestation of fear and hurt by a spirit of murder or hatred. Similarly, a spirit of rage may manifest passivity which effectively masks its true identity. The purpose, of course, is to throw the counselor off track and allow the spirit to escape detection.

I have learned to perceive the slightest evidence of demonic presence within a person. This perception functions only while in ministry. Thank God, I do not walk about seeing demonic manifestations in people I meet, nor do I look for them outside of the counseling setting. No one involved in our ministry is encouraged to see demons behind every tree and rock! Those who do may be in need of deliverance from an over sensitivity to demonic activity.

When I was first called into this ministry, the manifestations of unclean spirits were often quite violent. The violence was most always directed at the person ministering. It would rise up in the counselee and lash out at those seeking to help. Super-human strength on the part of the counselee would accompany these violent outbursts, often requiring four or five strong men to restrain an average size person. Usually there was a torrent of vile language, cursing God and all present. It was not uncommon for workers to be spit upon and struck by the counselee. Frequently rage and violence would be manifested in attempted self-destruction as the unclean spirits sought to destroy the counselee.

Since being led by the Holy Spirit into a non-violent ministry manifestations may be little more than the flexing of a muscle, the twitching of an eyelid or a smirk on the face. Other evidences include a rush of blood to the face causing the face to be flushed, the complete loss of color and the pallor of death, contortions of the body, sensations of heat or cold in the counselee's body, shortness of breath or choking and the presence of tension or pressure within the body of the counselee. The eyes of the counselee most often betray the presence of an unclean spirit as they reflect expressions of hatred, fear or other emotions.

Another clue to the presence of an unclean spirit is a feeling of fear or apprehension the counselee feels is not his own but is coming from another source. Sometimes there may be manifestations of pain especially within the head. On occasion, the unclean spirit will take control of the speech faculties to taunt those ministering. Generally, if the command to cease speaking is given, the unclean spirit will immediately become quiet. However, there are times when the spirit seems to hold some legal ground and will continue to speak. This seems to be a common manifestation among those whose lives are marked by strong rebellion.

The manifestations cited are to be expected in some degree when the strong man has been commanded into manifestation. Why call them into manifestation? First, an unclean spirit (as I understand what the Holy Spirit has taught us) must be stirred into action in order for it to leave. Secondly, it must use the faculties of the person indwelt in order to betray its presence. Finally, this is especially necessary when the counselee has been taught that Christians cannot be indwelt by an unclean spirit. When there is a manifestation, no doubt remains that an unclean spirit was present in his/her body and mind. Many skeptics have left a session confirmed believers in the possibility of unclean spirits indwelling the minds and bodies of Christians. Many ministers have seen demonic activity manifested in Spirit-filled members of their churches as they sat in on a deliverance session.

The departure of a spirit will generally be manifested. However, some do leave without a visible manifestation. When this happens the gift of discerning of spirits is invaluable. An early clue that a spirit is about to depart is tears in the eyes. A spirit may plead to remain, even promising not to torment the person anymore. There may be manifestations ranging from a simple relaxation to an explosive scream and contortioning of the body. Since unclean spirits are commissioned by Satan to steal, kill and destroy, (John 10:10) their final departure may be marked by some manifestation which seeks to fullfil that commission. However, in the context of non-violent deliverances in which angels are assigned to limit all forms of violence (especially toward those ministering) there need be no fear.

The most common manifestations observed in our ministry is that of the expulsion of air, coughing, burping, moaning, screaming and the relieving of inward tension and pressure. Frequently a person will report the sensation of a huge gas bubble rising from very deep within and then moving upward through the intestines, stomach, chest, throat and out through the mouth. It is also common for counselees to feel pressure in the head. Others report sensations of spirits leaving the finger tips, eyes, ears, nose and other parts of the body. There is no set pattern as each spirit is an entity capable of its own manifestation.

In most cases the departure of an unclean spirit is followed by a relaxation of the body and an inner peace. If tension remains, some part of the strong man's family may not have left or another strong man may be manifesting. Here is where the gift of discerning of spirits is needed. This gift reveals the true picture of what is occurring. A session should not be closed until all manifestations have ceased and there has been prayer for healing of the mind and body.

Practical Matters

At one time we ministered according to the teaching that there are seven areas of demonic control: rejection, fear, craving, bitterness, infirmity, anti-christ and death. The main point of this teaching was that only one spirit would be found in any given area and the casting out of that unclean spirit would bring complete deliverance.

During a particularly difficult session a spirit in one of those areas refused to leave. Finally, I commanded the unclean spirit to speak and reveal its legal ground by which it could defy the name of Jesus Christ. The unclean spirit responded, "I cannot leave for he will not let me go." I questioned the counselee as to why he would not allow the unclean spirit to leave. He shouted out, "I don't want it! I want it out!" I then commanded the unclean spirit to reveal who would not allow it to leave. The spirit replied "The one in authority over me will not allow me to leave."

Now I know there are those who believe and teach that one

should not converse with unclean spirits since they cannot speak the truth and it is degrading to talk with an unclean spirit. However, by this time the Holy Spirit had already taught us how to draw the truth from an unclean spirit. We found that we could ask a spirit if what it said would stand as absolute truth before the throne of the Living God and if the spirit was speaking the truth it would respond in the affirmative. If it had not spoken the truth it would say "No", submerge or leave. I have never been able to catch one in a lie once it so affirmed that it had spoken the truth. Occasionally we still verbally take a spirit before the Throne of God to confirm truth or falsehood.

Using this test, we found the unclean spirit had spoken the truth and it was commanded to cease manifesting (i.e. submerge). The stronger spirit was commanded to manifest which it did immediately and in great anger because it had been revealed. It promised retribution upon the lesser spirit for uncovering its presence. The stronger spirit was cast out and the lesser called up again and sent out also.

That is how we discovered there could be more than one spirit in each area and that unclean spirits tend to invade a person in family groupings. Each family grouping has a strong man in control. Through experience and continued study of scripture (especially concerning the spoiling of the strong man's house, Mt. 12:29 & Lk. 11:21,22,) we learned the family structure and how they function under the control of a strong man.

The structure we identified consisted of powers, rulers, works, controls, princes, principalities, dominions, mights, demons, wickedness in high places and the strong man. I do not say that this list is complete and certainly it is not infallible. All I can say is that this is what we feel the Holy Spirit opened to us.

For a considerable period of time we called each individual member of the family as they were revealed to us by the Holy Spirit. We would laboriously work our way through the list, commanding each one out, finishing with the strong man. Sometimes there was a response when each was commanded but not every time. As the awareness of the gift of discerning became stronger in Shirley, she was able to confirm the presence of the spirits. First, the strong man would be bound; then going through the list, casting out each family member until only the strong man remained; finally, he was cast out.

Eventually, the Holy Spirit led us to simply bind the strong man and command that he and his whole family leave the individual. Then

156

we wondered why the Holy Spirit led us the long way around. The rationale seemed to be that we now understood the reality of the family structure of unclean spirits and they knew that we possessed that knowledge. Therefore, there was no longer a need to identify each family member.

The Holy Spirit is faithful to identify the strong man. He will use the background information which has been gathered and, through discerning and word of knowledge, will reveal the strong man. The person in the command position should bind the strong man and his family and command them all to leave the counselee. I have found it effective to cut the roots and smash the strongholds of the demonic family with the Sword of the Spirit (i.e. the Word of God) in the counselee's conscious mind, sub-conscious mind, imagination, all areas of intelligence and reasoning, the senses, the emotional centers, the nervous communication system, glands, ganglion nerve of the stomach, blood system, respiratory system, muscles, cords and tendons. I then ask the heavenly Father to move the Sword of the Spirit from the crown of the head to the soles of the feet of the counselee cutting every root and smashing every stronghold in the mind and the body. As the cutting and smashing is being done all ranks and categories of the family are commanded out. When the manifestations cease the strong man and his family should be gone.

Why the Holy Spirit led me to call spirits from these specific area and not from others remains a mystery to me. There are times when other areas are pin-pointed, especially in the case of infirmities. If I try to merely command the exit of spirits from the mind and body of the individual some spirits seem to escape detection. I find then I must go back through the listing of areas given me in the first place. The Holy Spirit is the teacher and I am the student!

It is important that one be open to the leading of the Holy Spirit. Through His gifting it may be revealed that the unclean spirit has ceased to manifest and may be hidden somewhere in the counselee. A person with the gift of discerning of spirits will generally discern the spirit's presence. Often I sense a check in my own perception and continue to command the unclean spirit out. In most cases there will be a renewed manifestation. Do not give up too soon. It is better to command when nothing is there than to allow the spirit to go undetected. Each strong man and his family is dealt with in this same manner.

Perseverance and patience are needed when working in a deliverance session. Unclean spirits will employ every means possible to avoid being cast out. Their greatest desire is to convince the counselee that they do not exist and are not present. Confusion is a powerful tool so every effort will be made to convince the counselee that the manifestations and thoughts are his own. Once this is detected, the demon may then begin to threaten and project fear into the thought patterns. There may even be open threats of death to the counselee or the counselee's family. There is often a concerted effort by the unclean spirits to convince the counselee that everything happening is unreal and that those ministering are frauds.

A great deal has been said about commanding unclean spirits and there must be clarity concerning its exercise. Every command directed against an unclean spirit is spoken in the name of the Lord Jesus Christ and in the power of His shed blood. The one speaking in that name must know the person of the Lord Jesus Christ. To glibly call out in the name of the Lord Jesus Christ without a personal relationship with Him is like blowing into the wind. The words will go nowhere and accomplish nothing. The greater the knowledge of the person of the Lord Jesus Christ and the authority and power He confers to the believer, the greater will be the results.

We have seen the truth of this in sessions where people have sat in as learners. When given the opportunity to be in the command position the person has sat perplexed because the unclean spirit does not flee in terror. To the contrary, it may break out in laughter, hurling taunts and ridicule at the one ministering. You may be assured that the unclean spirits know the credentials brought into a session.

I have been asked numerous times why I do not lay hands upon the counselee when commanding spirits out. There are two reasons. First, it is my understanding that the laying on of hands is to impart something to someone. I do not see sufficient evidence in the scripture to warrant the laying on of hands to force something out of a person. Secondly, I rely upon the angels of God to restrain the counselee in order to prevent violence. My experience has been that when I do lay hands upon the counselee during a deliverance session, violence is usually the consequence. It is almost as if the angels move back and release the counselee's body. I do lay hands upon the counselee when explicitly directed by the Holy spirit and also for healing following a deliverance session.

The use of the gift of tongues and one's prayer language is desirable in a deliverance session. In the command position I seldom pray in the Spirit against unclean spirits. I hear reports of a "warring tongue" which is powerful against unclean spirits but I have not been led by the

Holy Spirit in this direction. I find that the unclean spirits understand English and respond to the commands given. I do encourage those observing or participating in any capacity to pray in the Spirit while I am commanding. There is power in those prayers. It is also an open channel for the Holy Spirit to give leading during a session.

It was stated earlier that the eyes often reveal the presence of an unclean spirit. Some believe and teach that without direct eye contact with the counselee unclean spirits cannot be cast out. I find that unclean spirits leave with eyes open or closed. It is the authority of the name of the Lord Jesus Christ and the power of His shed blood which drives out unclean spirits. Most counselees are more relaxed with their eyes closed. I choose not to make an issue of it in a deliverance session, allowing the counselee the freedom of choice.

Very often the counselee will express an inner urging to leave the counseling session or repeatedly needing to use the restroom. (Jokingly, we have identified this as the presence of a bathroom demon.) This is prompted by unclean spirits desiring to escape the authority about to be exercised against them. Every opportunity is seized by the unclean spirits to interrupt the flow of a deliverance session.

Often it seems as if some person is present, hindering the session, yet that person is miles away. We have identified the hinderance as the work of a familiar spirit, an unclean spirit assigned by Satan to travel with an individual. When such a spirit is present the commands seem to bounce off the counselee with no effect. It is as if a wall has been erected between the counselor and counselee. Likewise, the gifts of discerning of spirits and word of knowledge and word of wisdom are hindered. Everything seems to grind to a halt.

At that point we have found it effective to cut every tie, cord and line of communication from the counselee and the person who seems to be represented. Then the familiar spirit is commanded out of the building. To assure its departure, we ask the heavenly Father to assign angels to escort the spirit out, along with any other hindering spirits. In most cases the deliverance session is then freed to continue.

A deliverance session can often be likened to a chess game with move and countermove between the counselor and the spirits within the counselee. However, in this chess game a great deal is at stake. The very personality and life of the counselee is involved. Therefore, deliverance is never a parlor game or a ministry that is exercised lightly. It is a time of war - spiritual warfare!

PRAYER - OPEN A SESSION

(Model Prayer)

The following is a model of what we usually pray at the beginning of each session. This should not be followed rigidly. Each counselor should develop his/her own prayer as led by the Holy Spirit but this will give some guidelines.

Dear Heavenly Father, as we come now to minister before you, I ask that this building and property be completely filled with your holy angels, that they circle round about, over and under, that all of our loved ones and all circumstances represented here today come under your divine protection and the protection of the shed blood of the Lord Jesus Christ. I ask that each of us and all our loved ones be encircled now with Your heavenly angels.

In the authority of the Name of the Lord Jesus Christ and the power of His shed blood I now bind the satanic kingdom on earth just as it is bound in heaven. I also bind it especially that no unclean spirits shall be sent into this place for any purpose whatsoever. Nor shall they be sent to any other place or any other person because of the circumstances here this day.

In that same authority and power I now bind every unclean spirit in order that there shall be no violence manifested here today in any way nor shall there be any violence manifested against any other person or in any other place because of the circumstances here today.

In that same authority and power I now bind every unclean spirit in order that there shall be no interference with the work of the Holy Spirit here this day. If there is to be any movement of unclean spirits here today, it shall be out of here to that place that Jesus Christ alone wills they shall go.

I ask now, Father, that angels be assigned to assure that all these bindings are in place and to place any other needed bindings.

Father, we now bring our minds and wills into complete agreement with Your mind and will and in agreement with the perfect mind and will of the Lord Jesus Christ.

Father, if we should fall into error today as we are ministering, I ask that You either stop us, correct us, or grant us the discerning to see the error ourselves that we might correct it. We refuse to serve the enemy in any capacity. We serve only to the praise, glory and honor of the Person and the Name of the Lord Jesus Christ.

Father, I ask now that everything of our flesh that might hinder the work of the Holy Spirit to be stripped away that we might take to ourselves those priestly garments to come right into the center of the holy place of Your will.

Father, I ask now for the division of the conscious and sub-conscious mind of ..... in order that there might be that deep probing by the Holy Spirit. I ask that angels be assigned to assure that this has been accomplished. I ask that the Holy Spirit take control now of the imagination, conscious and sub-conscious mind of ..... that there might be that deep probing of the sub-conscious mind to uncover any hidden work of the enemy whereby bondages may have come upon .....

Now in the authority of the name of Jesus Christ and the power of His shed blood I take the sword of the Spirit, which is the Holy Word. I wield that sword now to sever and close all avenues of communication between unclean spirits present here now with the principalities, powers and rulers of darkness in this world and spiritual wickedness in high places assigned to this geographic area. I sever and close all avenues of communication with witches covens, occult workers and satanic workers of the black arts. I sever and close all avenues of communication with Satan himself in order that all unclean spirits present be isolated from all communication with evil sources.

In that same authority and power I bind all unclean spirits present to every command given in the authority of the name of the Lord Jesus Christ and the power of His

161

shed blood. Every unclean spirit shall be obedient and in submission to every command given in that authority and power. Now, Father, I ask that angels be assigned to assure this has been accomplished and to place other needed bindings.

Father, we now open ourselves to all needed gifting by the Holy Spirit and ask that the Holy Spirit be in control of all circumstances here today.

Father, we give all praise, glory and honor unto the Person and the Name of the Lord Jesus Christ. Amen.

PRAYER - BREAK THE CURSE

OF

THE SINS OF THE FATHERS

The following is a sample prayer to be used in order to break any and all bondages which may have come down upon a person because of sins committed his/her forefathers in previous generations.

Dear Heavenly Father, I come before You now to confess the sins of my fathers whereby curses, iniquities, and whoredoms may have come down upon me and my generations.

Father, these are the sins: the sin of adultery, fornication, incest, sexual immorality, sexual deviations, homosexuality, lesbianism, unrighteousness, wickedness, maliciousness, covetousness, idolatry, sedition, heresy, witchcraft, jealousy, envy, wrath, strife, murder, hatred, lasciviousness, stealing, drunkenness, extortion, deceit, argumentativeness, whisperings, backbiting, boasting, pride, false witness, lying, rebellion and all evil desires.

(NOTE: The sins listed in this prayer have been drawn from the following Bible passages: Rom. 1:29-31;I Cor. 6:9-10; and Gal.5:19.)

Father, I confess these now as sins of my fathers. I also confess my own involvement in some of these sins. I ask now that You forgive me and I accept that forgiveness. I now forgive my forefathers and I ask that You forgive those sins. I accept that forgiveness. Now in the Name of the Lord Jesus Christ I lift every curse, every iniquity and every whoredom that has come down upon me and my generations. I lift them off now and I thank my Lord and Savior Jesus Christ. Amen.

(At the close of the prayer the strong man of the curse of the sins of the fathers is to be cast out.)

PRAYER TO CLOSE A SESSION

This prayer, as all others, is a model prayer. Each person is to develop their own prayer covering those things which are felt to be essential. This prayer sets some basic elements which may be included in your prayer.

Lord Jesus Christ, I ask now that you manifest your presence to . . . . in whatever manner he/she may know your presence. And now I speak healing to the mind. Every ravage and tear that has been made we now bring under the healing virtue of the Lord Jesus Christ. To every wounded memory we speak healing. Lord Jesus Christ, if there is any incident from out of the past requiring correction or healing, we ask now that you take . . . . by the hand and lead him/her through the incident as you heal and correct. And now we command the imagination, conscious mind, sub-conscious mind, all areas of intelligence and reasoning to receive their healing and be healed to the glory of the name of the Lord Jesus Christ. We speak that same healing now to the physical body that it receive its healing to the glory of the name of the Lord Jesus Christ. I ask now that the Holy Spirit move into every area that has been vacated by unclean spirits, that . . . . never be the house empty but to be filled with the presence of the Holy Spirit and the Word of God. I ask now that warring angels be assigned to watch over every area until healing is total and complete. I ask now that the conscious and sub-con-

163

scious mind come back into their normal relationship and function.

(NOTE: At this point it is well to ask the heavenly Father to loose whatever the counselor feels may be needed for the welfare of the counselee and further healing. We make it a point to ask that heavenly angels be assigned to go with the counselee and to stay with that person until no longer needed. We feel it is important that the counselee have special protection after a deliverance or inner-healing session.)

Father, we give all the praise, glory and honor unto the name and person of the Lord Jesus Christ for all that has been done here this day. Amen.

CHAPTER 10

A SOLDIER OF THE CROSS!

(VISION OF THE ARMY)

It is now decision time. If you have carefully read the preceding pages, you now realize this is a subject requiring a decision. It is not possible to remain neutral and hope some future scientific breakthrough will explain away the biblical doctrine of demons. By now you are either convinced of the validity of demonic activity in the world today or you must discount the record of scripture and the testimony of the saints.

This final word is an appeal to those who are convinced and believe we are in a war to the finish. The people of God are being called to battle. It is no longer permitted for the Christian to sit on the sidelines, unconcerned or incapacitated, while a few knowledgeable and inundated stalwarts carry the fight to the enemy. During World War II, the United States was continuously urged to a total war effort. We were encouraged to be involved at some level of participation commensurate with our abilities. Even children were urged to participation by buying Saving Stamps, writing letters, growing victory gardens, etc. This war is no less demanding of the citizens of the Kingdom of God and its consequences are eternal.

During a time of critical assessment of the apathy of the church toward spiritual warfare the Lord impressed upon me a picture of worldly warfare. It was made clear to me the picture or vision was in terms of conventional rather than nuclear warfare.

I saw point men hidden from view of the enemy. Their assignment was to get as close to the enemy as possible without being detected. From that vantage point they were to relay back to the main army all possible information concerning the enemy. These men were in a most precarious position. If detected, they faced the likelihood of destruction. The men were combat veterans and well trained. This was no place for raw recruits.

At a distance behind them was another line of men occupying entrenchments. It served as a first line of defense to which the point men might retreat should they be detected by the enemy. Hopefully, this line would hold off an attack until help could arrive. This, too, was a vulnerable position and was manned mostly by veteran officers and men.

165

Further back stood the main army. It was made up of veteran and newly arrived officers and men. Some had experienced battle while others were yet to face battle. Some of the officers were disgruntled. Perhaps their advancement in rank had not been as rapid as desired or they may have been passed over for others less experienced. Some of the soldiers, too, felt they had not been dealt with fairly. The dread and anticipation of battle hung over all concerned.

Farther back were the supply units, busily bringing supplies to the advance troops. Here again, there was a mix of veterans and raw recruits. There were dedicated officers and the disgruntled.

At a distant point were the training commands where the raw recruits come to be trained for combat. Some were "gung-ho, Rambo" types itching to get into battle while others, resigned to their lot in life, simply followed along. Here again, many frustrated officers only put in their time. That frustration came down upon those who served under them.

Lastly, I saw the "hurrah" groups. Their task was to pep up the troops, bring men into the army, sell war bonds and hype the home groups into support of the warfare. Some could not meet the standards needed for warfare and served in this capacity. Many were celebrities admired by the crowds.

Having seen this vision of a conventional army with its dedicated members and its disgruntled participants along with its trained and untrained leaders, it seemed the Lord was saying:

> "My son, this is a picture of My church on earth. It is a rag-tag army at best but I use every part of it for My purposes, even the hurrah groups! It is made up of veteran leaders and men/women together with those lacking true commitment. Many possess knowledge of spiritual warfare while others are little more than raw recruits. Some, with varying degrees of knowledge and dedication, are training others for battle. I have a few who serve as point men - you are one of those. You face the enemy day in and day out. There are times when you confront the enemy face to face. It is the responsibility of those on point to inform the church of the strength and activities of the enemy. Your's is a vulnerable position; the enemy hates you with a passion. There are a few churches like that first line of defense to which you may

retreat in the event of attack. They are but a few but that is all that I have. I desire a dedicated, trained army for the end times. I have called. Who will answer?"

I am not so foolish as to expect everyone to devote themselves full time to a ministry of deliverance and inner-healing. However, without reservation I urge every believer to be deeply and continuously involved in those works that bring healing and deliverance to people held captive by Satan. There is a vital part each one can have in this warfare and we need to be "about our Father's business."

In the first place, you can begin now to resist the devil and to yield yourself to God. This alone will gain many victories and bring a new vitality to your Christian life. It is also possible you will discover the root cause of some prevailing sin pattern is actually demonic. Should this be the case, there is no need to panic. You have become aware of the enemy's tactics and you are now equipped to do battle. Do not hesitate to seek the help of other mature Christians in the warfare. Do not give up, you shall overcome. Greater is He that is in you (the Lord Jesus Christ) then he that is in the world (that old serpent, the devil.)

Begin to pray, asking the Lord to make you aware of the needs around you. You will likely be amazed to discover how many hurting, desperate people are in your circle of acquaintances. You are not powerless before their great need. God has given you great and precious promises and has put weapons that are powerful in your grasp. These weapons are mighty to the tearing down of satanic strongholds and overcoming spiritual wickedness in high places. You can be an instrument of deliverance and inner-healing as you give yourself to being led by the Holy Spirit.

There are undoubtedly many, just like yourself, concerned about the needs but uncertain what to do. Ask the Holy Spirit to begin to uncover each to the other so that you will all realize you are not alone in the battle. Get a network of praying people organized to go to prayer at a moment's notice. This alone will bring radical changes in the community God has placed you in.

Begin to pray for the spiritual leadership of your area. Many are truly God's choice servants but for a great variety of reasons they are wary of spiritual warfare. Their hearts are towards God and His people but their heads are filled with doubt concerning the reality of demonic activity. Fervent, believing prayer can bring about great change among the spiritual leaders, breaking down resistent attitudes.

Because of these prevailing attitudes, most inner-healing and deliverance ministries have had to work as agencies outside the regular church organizations. We, ourselves, have had to form a non-profit foundation in which to carry on our ministry. You can financially support such ministries and undergird them with constant prayer. Satan would like to bring all such ministries to a halt but he cannot prevail in the face of victorious prayer and the support of God's people.

You can make choices - become involved, avoid the issue because of fear and ignorance, declare it all to be superstitious poppy-cock or even become aligned with God's enemies. Satan will help you along to any decision except to become involved in the warfare. He knows he cannot win but he will not stop.

We know we cannot lose, so why do we hesitate? Beloved, we are kings and priests unto Jesus Christ; we have available all power in heaven and earth. We can be overcomers! God is calling, the enemy is working, the power is available - IT IS TIME FOR WAR!!

BIBLIOGRAPHY

Bible references are taken from the King James Version unless otherwise stated.

Griffin, <u>The Mystery of Iniquity</u>, Charis Life Ministries, Portland, Oregon.

Edersheim, Alfred, D.D.,Ph.D., <u>Bible History</u>, Vol. II, History of Judah and Israel, William B. Eerdmans Publishing Co., Grand Rapids, Michigan.

Latourette, Kenneth Scott, <u>A History of Christianity</u>, Harper & Brothers Publishers, New York, New York, 1953.

C.L. Barnhart, Editor in Chief, Jess Stein, Managing Editor, <u>The American College Dictionary</u>, Random House, Inc., New York, New York, 1960.

Unger, Merril F., <u>Unger's Bible Dictionary</u>, Moody Press, Chicago, Illinois, 1957.

Solberg, Frank O., <u>You Can Be Free</u>, Nampa Offset Printing Co., Nampa, Idaho.

* * * * *

OTHER BOOKS AVAILABLE THROUGH SOLID ROCK BOOKS, INC.
979 Young Street, Suite E
Woodburn, OR 97071
(503) 981-0705

Becoming A Vessel Of Honor In The Master's Service, By Dr. Rebecca Brown, MD. The PURPOSE of this book is to help you UNDERSTAND the rapidly expanding world of the occult so that you can cleanse yourself from any involvement in it. UNDERSTAND the "sin nature" and learn how to control it. This book contains SECRET SATANIC WAR PLANS previously not found in print. It reveals how the followers of Satan are openly confronting the followers of Jesus Christ. You must LEARN the key to spiritual power *before* you need it! A MUST FOR EVERY CHRISTIAN!

For Many Shall Come In My Name, by Ray Yungen. Fresh insights on the New Age Movement. Did you know that modern New Age Movement was described in both the New and Old Testaments? Are you aware that one of the fastest growing techniques sweeping the medical field is based on occultism? Learn how the fields of teaching, healing and counseling are being profoundly affected.

Strongman's His Name. What's His Game? by Jerry & Carol Robeson. A Scriptural, Balanced, Uplifting approach to present-day SPIRITUAL WARFARE. Instead of binding symptoms we bind the 16 strongmen mentioned BY NAME in the Bible. It TEACHES how to zero in and identify the Strongman. It INSTRUCTS how to bind the enemy and loose the Power of God. It PROVIDES instant recognition when and where the enemy is attacking our life and the lives of those around us.